"In his spirited debut novel, *School Board*, Mike Freedman delivers a rousing tale of politics and politicking, introducing the world to the noblest crusader any side of the Mississippi: Tucker 'Catfish' Davis. With the comic heroism of Don Quixote and the clever irreverence of Huckleberry Finn, 'Catfish' will capture your heart, win your vote and take you to the prom. Freedman has written a love letter to the city of Houston, the great Gulf Coast, the legacy of Huey 'Kingfish' Long and the long-lost tradition of American Populism. Darkly comic and charming as heck, *School Board*, announces Mike Freedman as one of our brightest new literary stars."—AMBER DERMONT, author of the *New York Times* bestseller, *The Starboard Sea*, and *Damage Control*

"Into the riotous cavalcade of great American literary characters tumbles a new class clown, Tucker 'Catfish' Davis, high school senior and aspiring politician. One part Ignatius J. Reilly from *A Confederacy of Dunces*, one part Hazel Motes from *Wise Blood*, and several parts Willie Stark from *All the King's Men*, Catfish Davis is a singular presence on the page. Mike Freedman hasn't just written the funniest book about a school board election, he's written the kind of David-and-Goliath story that gets all of us 'little people' cheering and laughing in equal measure."—DAVID ABRAMS, author of Fobbit

"Tucker Davis, the protagonist of this energetic novel, joins a select group of great American characters—Huck Finn, Ignatius J. Reilly, and John Yossarian, among others—who are as indelible and unique as they are hilarious and flawed."—JEREMY JACKSON, author of *Life at These Speeds* and *I Will Not Leave You Comfortless*

"*School Board* is a total joy to read, as full of sass and subversive brass as its 18-year-old hero, the political neophyte and Houston school board candidate Tucker 'Catfish' Davis. It's a rare kid who's willing to take on a big-city establishment, but Catfish does it with gusto, opening minds and antagonizing the powers-that-be to delicious effect. We need more of that old-time populist spirit! And more books like Mike Freedman's romp of a debut novel. I hope *School Board* is the first of many more to come from this gifted young writer."—BEN FOUNTAIN, author of National Book Critics Circle Award winner *Billy Lynn's Long Halftime Walk* and *Brief Encounters with Che Guevara*

School Board

School Board

A novel by Mike Freedman

To the Great Bill Broyles,
I hope you enjoy this comic tale set in your own Bayou City. Thank you for lending the way & showing us post-9/11 vets how to act, lead, & write!
Every Kid A King!
[illegible]

CHIN MUSIC PRESS

2014 | Broken Levee Books
An imprint of Chin Music Press | Seattle

Publisher:
Chin Music Press
2621 24th Ave W
Seattle, WA 98199-3407

www.chinmusicpress.com

ISBN: 978-0-9887693-8-0

First [1] edition

Book design: Linda Ronan
Cover illustration: Jessica Lynn Bonin

Printed in the USA

Library of Congress cataloging-in-publication data available.

For my brothers Jeff and Dan
and
To the generation of post-9/11 dreamer brothers who were crazy enough to sally forth overseas

"You may be right and they may be every bit as intelligent as you say, but I'd feel a whole lot better about them if just one of them had run for sheriff once."

—Sam Rayburn to Lyndon B. Johnson in response to President Kennedy's Cabinet selection, in David Halberstam's *The Best and the Brightest*

If you're ever in Houston, you better walk right;
You better not gamble, you better not fight,
Or the sheriff will grab you, and the boys will bring you down.
The next thing you know, you're penitentiary bound.

—"The Midnight Special"

Bayou down, down, down below swollen gulf blown clouds lanced by downtown scaled-glass skyscrapers beat the beat between banks of an undredged world. East of downtown, water flowed to a ship channel out to the gulf. To the west, cypress and jungle vine brown-green hundreds of feet up rose in humid heat to meet in a canopy, swallowing lengths of the muddy water fifty-mile cut. Light escaped on flotillas of young alligator gars, the old gars beneath at rest with the alligators, sharing the water with cottonmouths, blue herons, soft-shell turtles, and bats swooping on mosquito colonies of Buffalo Bayou.

The lone boat paddled west, upstream. Fighting the same current, a manatee likewise out of place swam, a bend behind. The paddle for both was easier because of the drought. No one disturbed either, the ignored bayou a drainage facility recalled only in flood.

Up through the undredged world, citizens of the Bayou City moved in the other direction. Never a town to look back, new pioneers explored waters and lands and space to be tomorrow's history. Begat in a coastal swamp, it grew in a fever, lost in a fever, and always rediscovered in a fever.

Named after the greatest Texan of all time, Houston, was Houston. One day, legend had it, the great General Houston would remount and ride again to reclaim history.

One

He was the Last Populist.

In the last year of the twentieth-century, in a country full of populists, he laid claim to the last. Jefferson High School Senior Class President Tucker Davis would die without any of the breed left to bury him.

So on the spring morning when the criminal trial of Louisiana Governor Bobby Boudreaux commenced, Tucker Davis—last in the populist line stretching from Huey "Kingfish" Long through his brother Earl K. Long—brought news of his own funeral to the little folks of his old elementary school. He removed his tan fedora at the fenced entrance to the paved track looping around the school playground. Wavy chestnut hair, barely restrained in the wide-brimmed hat, spilled out in a shock of curls. In a ballooned baby face unmarked by facial hair, Tucker's ornery brown eyes bugged out beneath the unruly curl, searching the school for signs of a fight on behalf of little folks. He paid no heed to the rows of planted young oak trees or the bike rack in the design of a tennis shoe outside the renovated library, his eyes blind to all the abundant additions that exemplified Memorial Elementary School as a district paragon. Overlooking the new red goal posts at each end of the field, which smelled of cut grass, he focused on one forgotten patch of dead grass and dirt the size of a picnic blanket in the middle of the soccer field. Nothing's changed, Tucker thought, they're still short-changing the little folks.

On the playground, three children shot a basketball off a glass backboard. Tucker raised his index finger to Jefferson High School Senior Class Vice President Elliott Taylor, who studied for biology inside his pickup truck, and headed toward the uncovered basketball court. The bowlegs progressed forward in sideward alternating tacks, as if each leg divined a quest in the other direction. The rest of Tucker's gangly frame dragged behind in tow, a plow in reverse zigzagging across the field.

The concrete basketball court absorbed the heat from the climbing sun. A map of the world painted in varying colors for each country and labeled in black covered the length of the court. Inside half court, Tucker stopped at the far end of the world on a country in yellow. From Saudi Arabia he waited on the crowd.

It was a game of cutthroat, every kid for himself. With the arrival of Tucker, the three children stopped clanking shots from the three-point line and played closer to the goal. The tight net made it easy to control the ball as it rustled through and dropped gently below. After every basket, the scorer shot free throws. Each of the three scraped and shot to be the first to score twenty-one points. Tucker waited for an opportunity on the edge of the court, his legs set in an incorrect shooting position of a right angle.

As the middle-sized boy in a Cub Scout uniform cut hard to the goal for the winning basket, he dribbled the ball off his left foot and sent it straight at Tucker. The ball bounced twice like a pinball in the open jaws of the bowlegs. It rolled to a stop. None of the four moved. Black beads strung on the shirt pocket of the Cub Scout uniform dangled in the sun. His eyes sizing the audience, Tucker's hand slid down his side and unbuttoned the lowest button on the front right side of his Kingfish uniform—a bronze double-breasted suit. Leaving the basketball on the ground, Tucker shot first.

"Call me crazy," Tucker said pointing the fedora at the biggest kid. "But call me Catfish." Tucker shifted the aimed fedora to the Cub Scout. "How old are y'all?"

"Seven and a half," the Cub Scout said. "Pass the—"

"That's a great age, seven and a half. Sure beats kindergarten, don't it? Hell, I'm eighteen and I still hold a grudge against kindergarten and my teacher putting me in the slow reading group and all. But that didn't stop me any from becoming president of the senior class."

"I want my basketball back."

"Always either a raw deal or no deal. I would be cynical too if I were your age and trying to play the game."

Across the small patch of dead grass and dirt, Elliott charged toward the court, his blonde hair flopping on top of his six-and-a-half-foot, all-district basketball frame. Three aged oak trees bearded with gray scraggly moss hung over the edge of the court adjacent to the orderly rows of young oak trees. Under the mossy oaks, Tucker considered the fate of little folks as if among a gathering of tribal elders. Was it possible for a kid to still rise from nothing to class president? Before Tucker were the little folks of Houston, forgotten masses on a forgotten playground, and no one held accountable for it. With no populist in their government to fight for little folks and against corruption, Tucker saw the dust bowl substituted for a soccer field in this wasteland. To the crowd of three second-graders, Tucker summoned, "How long have y'all waited?"

The clock on the wall said eight. Classes on Election Day at Jefferson High School began in twenty minutes. "Hey boss," Elliott said running up, "we need to get to school for Election Day. You promised just a minute here."

"I didn't come here to give a speech about promises unfulfilled," Tucker said, hands outstretched and offered to the three dust bowl refugees. "Y'all who have come here every day to school, across dying fields and under scarred oaks. And y'all aren't the first generation to gather under these oaks in disappointment and wait. With your tomorrow traded away for today's bribes of candy and kickball games—the books they promised that never came. No, y'all don't need no lecture from Catfish reminding y'all about the way they treat us little folks."

"They're just kids," Tucker heard a voice say. Tucker scanned the sweaty faces of the three second-graders and stopped on the smallest boy who dipped his head side to side. Tucker remembered that nervousness well from the days when he alone battled the elementary school administration and rallied little folks. Tucker lunged toward the smallest boy and fired a going-over-the-trenches stare at him to let him know they fought under fire together. Behind Tucker, Elliott pleaded, "They're just kids."

"Hell, I know you are just a kid and ain't old enough to vote. I ain't running for anything or asking for your vote. But that don't mean every kid ain't a king. I know they're always feeding you about how you are too young. They told Huey Long the same thing when he was trying to make every man a king. But you, you, and you," Tucker said, his hat jabbing the air at each child's heart, "ain't too young to attend this tax-paying school district of ours. And one ain't ever too young to have a say. Them same folks is always saying, when I'm fighting for us on account of something, 'Tuck Davis, he's just a kid.' Damn right old Tuck Catfish Davis is just a kid. The kid who made rich folks share some of that wealth. The kid who saw to it that working folks of the Jefferson High School Class of '99 fed at the trough too. Crackers and kids of color alike. And who kicked the moneychangers out of the temple even when the administration suits tried to put Catfish's bullhead in a noose? Tuck Davis, that's who."

Tucker pulled out his yellow tie with white polka dots and wiped the light coat of slimy perspiration from his white face and tucked it back in between his suit and shirt. The game of cutthroat had turned into an unwanted game of freeze for the three motionless children. There was a rise in Tucker, a rise pushing his eyes out to the crowd of three second-graders as the rise of words to rally the crowd stirred out of his mouth.

"Dammit if Catfish ain't going to lick them again, even if it takes all the milk money y'all and the other hard-traveling people of this school have got. Because we're going to see some seats put on those playground swings for a change."

"Those are monkey bars, Tucker," Elliott said, "they're not supposed to have seats. We're going to be late if we don't get going."

"Dammit if we don't start with their political office seats!" Tucker bellowed. "I don't just aim to sit in the seat we're going to take from them. I aim to last swinging as we roll out other new bills of change for the little folks! And when y'all fall down off that new swing, y'all will be able to get a pass to the new clinic. And when y'all are out of the clinic, y'all are going to still have a quarter in your pocket for a cold Dr Pepper and a pack of baseball trading cards!"

The smallest boy reached down into the pockets of his blue jeans. He pulled out a worn dollar and two quarters. Tucker took it all in: tears at the corners of the boy's blue eyes, the torn pants, and the tug-of-war work calluses on the little hand as the boy extended the donation into the hat. Tucker looked down at each of the faces, wishing he could pull a rabbit from his fedora and bring some momentary happiness to their hardscrabble existence. They had a long slog ahead, Tucker knew from experience, even with a populist now in their corner fighting for them.

"It takes a worried kid," Tucker said. He nodded at the children so they knew Tuck Davis heard their unease. "Don't think y'all don't have a dog in this fight. He's called Catfish. I might be the Last Populist, but I ain't dead yet."

The biggest kid bent down and unzipped a pocket on the side of his tennis shoe. The big coin flashed in the sun as the boy placed it in the collection. A bag of Mexican silver from a lost mine would not have moved Tucker more. Tucker cursed that he did not have a copy of Huey Long's autobiography to autograph and give to the boy.

"It's the kid's lucky fifty-cent piece, Tuck," Elliott said, taking a step forward from behind Tucker. Elliott put his hand on Tucker's back, standing a good half foot taller than his friend. "Are you trying to get us arrested? I should've known as soon as I picked you up and saw you in that suit and hat."

"We're fighting to make the ruling few of this city share," Tucker said. Elliott clapped twice and turned back to the truck. Tucker held up the coin for all to see and transferred the coin and the other money to his jacket breast pocket. "If every kid in this greatest of all cities is cut from the same stock as you three, the fat cats don't have a prayer strong enough to save their crony network. Not a damn prayer. Not against your grit. And I'll be damned if there ain't a finer quality out there than toughness. Toughness and dreams founded this city, raised it right out of the swamp. Sometimes you got to get down in the muck and muck about. That's why folks call me Catfish." Tucker returned the fedora to his head and tilted the front brim back to release the shock of curls onto his forehead. He passed through them and said, "Takes a worried kid."

The three second-graders left the ball on the court as Tucker and Elliott crossed the field. Biggest in the lead, they sprinted over to the gym teacher who had begun setting up jump rope stations on the far end of the track. They jumped and pointed at a white pickup truck parked on the other side of the track.

Inside Elliott's white pickup, Tucker pressed his face against the window and smiled at the excitement of the three gritty second-graders who jumped up and down to spread the populist message to an adult on the far side of the track. Tucker shook his head at the school where he had met Elliott thirteen years before and said, "This ought to be a hell of a place to go to school." Tucker turned away from the window and repeated the line three more times as Elliott shifted gears and drove past the front of the school and the new marquee that read 1998-1999 NATIONAL EXEMPLARY SCHOOL.

"Miss Henry pulled me aside last week to talk about politics," Elliott said. He drove east on Memorial Drive through Bunker Hill Valley Village, a valley of million-dollar homes bunched on the edge of the road.

"Talk politics with you? I'm the president of the class."

"She pulled me aside so I could advise you to keep your fingers out of the sophomore and junior class elections today at the high school," Elliott said. "Miss Henry doesn't like you. That's why there is a new rule counting ballots cast as only eighty-five percent of the total points, and teacher-decided student merit as the other fifteen percent for student council positions. Be glad Miss Henry didn't drive by and see you frightening those kids with your rabble-rousing. If she catches you interfering today on Election Day, she will go straight to Dr. Green."

"Don't you think I know what Miss Henry will do? Let her talk to the bosses while I go straight to the people," Tucker said, trying to wave his fedora inside the truck. "I can't stomach another one of her lectures on the evil of demagogues. One day teachers like Miss Henry are going to get good government—and they ain't going to like it! What does she know about government anyway?"

"She's our government teacher."

"Ain't a politician. She doesn't have any place in politics advising the student council. That new election law of hers is against everything I've fought for. All that's missing is a poll tax on the people. A kid can't even find himself an election to run in these days. You saw this morning with your own eyes; ain't no one out there defending and raining down change for the little folks. What are the people of this school district going to do when we graduate?"

"Who are you taking to prom?"

"Been so busy running it, I hadn't given it much thought," Tucker said. He thought about which girls might not reject him. "I might ask Dunazade Shari."

Elliott laughed. "Of course, there is still the fact that you have yet to speak a word to Duna in the two years since she transferred to Jefferson."

His vice president had a point about approaching Duna, Tucker conceded to himself. Duna had referred once to her Persian background in class. But Tucker knew all too well he did not know the first thing about Persian populists or politics, even where this Persia place was located on the map or what its little folks were like.

Elliott pulled the truck past the red and white Mustang statue into the senior parking lot of Jefferson High School. "Only four more weeks until we're finally out of here. The little folks are going to miss you, Catfish."

"I reckon four weeks ain't enough time to change anything for them. If only there was more time to fight for them. You know Catfish would."

"We know," Elliott said, parking his truck in the back corner of the senior lot. Students smoked cigarettes behind the pharmacy thirty feet away on the other side of the street. In the space next to Elliott and Tucker, four boys huddled in front of a truck grossly elevated with tires that appeared to be designed for off-roading in the Baja 100. Elliott pulled out his vocabulary list from his backpack and reviewed it against the steering wheel. Tucker dismounted from the truck.

"I'm going to go see what the candidates are up to," Tucker said.

"Have you finished your paper on the white whale for Mrs. Bridge?"

Tucker strode across the parking lot toward the new auditorium. A plastic black and white banner hanging over the front entrance of the auditorium declared it WALKER B. MOORE DAY. Neither sophomore-year nor junior-year candidates campaigned in the front courtyard.

"What's with the costume? I thought the talent show was next week," a joker heckled from a group Tucker passed.

Tucker shook the hand of the joker and said, "Election Day, Senior Class President Tuck Davis." Tucker loosened his tie and headed for the main office. Few campaign posters dotted the halls. Tucker stopped in front of the most prominent poster for class president. It proclaimed in red and silver glitter: BE REALLY COOL, VOTE WHITNEY TOOLE! Surely, Tucker thought, this was not the successor to: SHARE OUR WEALTH, VOTE CATFISH DAVIS. What a platform and campaign that was. Blew in like a hurricane hitched to a freight train.

First bell broke off the memory of the Tucker Davis whistle-stop tour of a year ago. Brokered deals and united cliques had formed the Share Our Wealth Coalition, a coalition with no equal in Jefferson High School history: jocks, nerds, artists, smokers, journalists, the band, and any orphans hopped the freight train. Tucker parlayed the coalition signatures into a petition to end water's long monopoly, bringing the first Dr Pepper machine to the school.

The conductor of the Share Our Wealth Coalition edited the morning announcements handed to him by school secretary Mrs. Bryce. As usual, much editing needed to be done by Tucker to infuse the material from school principal Dr. Green with political content. Pleased with his announcements edits, Tucker switched the microphone on, the second bell signaling the start of first period long passed.

— - — - —

Walker B. Moore checked his beeper and waited for the announcer to finish before continuing his speech to Miss Henry's government class.

"And if y'all don't like any of the candidates on the ballot, write in who y'all want in office. This is Election Day. So vote in the kid y'all want, not who the kingmakers think merits it. Lastly, Senior Awards Night is tonight at seven in the auditorium," concluded the voice from the PA system box over Walker's head.

Walker noticed the announcer made no mention of the official dedication at Senior Awards Night of the new Walker B. Moore Auditorium, or of Walker B. Moore Day at Jefferson High School. The interruption over, Walker resumed thanking Miss Henry and her government class for their kind introduction. Over the speaker, the folk song "House of the Rising Sun" closed the announcements by interrupting Walker again.

Walker raised his voice to speak over a verse on prostitution. "It really is an honor to be here as your guest in a classroom where I once sat as you sit today. By the looks of it, probably at the same desks. And what an honor to have a day dedicated to me at my old school. The school where my son, Chuck Moore, who many of you know and are friends with, now also goes to school. I never would have thought this possible thirty-five years ago when I was a senior in the very first Mustang graduating class at Jefferson High School, the Class of '64. All I cared about then was not failing so I could play Mustang baseball. I still remember that for one of our senior class pranks, one of your own Houston city councilmen, Skip Brammer—"

"Tell us, President Moore," Miss Henry said, "a little bit about the civic responsibilities of being both an elected representative and serving as the board-appointed president of the Memorial Independent School District school board. In anticipation of your visit to our class today, some of the students were asking me last week what it is you do. I have been encouraging them to become active in local politics since most are now eighteen and eligible to vote in the upcoming school board election. I know you are unopposed this year, but maybe you could win some future votes talking to us about your position."

"Commitment. Character." Disappointed that Miss Henry halted his story about the black shoe polish Skip Brammer applied to the crotch of the Mustang statue his senior year, Walker stumbled for words to dignify the presidency. "Integrity. Selfless devotion to cause. Above all, loyalty," Walker said catching sight of the LOYALTY poster of two remora fish attached to a shark beside the classroom clock. "Loyalty to do the right thing in making decisions benefiting the entire school district. This is the biggest responsibility any school board president faces during his time in office. Not unlike the tough decisions I make every day at Synergy as president of Synergy Capital & Trade. Also, control. One needs control—"

The classroom door swung open. Walker and the few remaining students paying attention swiveled to see Tucker shuffle in. At the sight of the most troublesome little league player Walker had ever coached, Walker jerked and put a steadying hand out, which landed on the head of a sleeping student.

Tucker Davis. The rambling, nonsensical voice on the loudspeaker was *his*. The mutinous clown had traded the Red Devils baseball uniform of Walker's team for a ridiculous suit and fedora hat. Walker gasped. His hands tumbled summersaults in front of his chest in the air he tried to breathe. "What . . . was I . . . saying?"

"Let's open it up for questions. President Moore is a busy man as both a school board president and as a senior executive at the largest company in Houston. Try to ask thoughtful, specific questions pertaining to government and economics," Miss Henry said. "Yes, Duna?"

A petite, black-haired girl half the size of Walker stood up. She held a yellow notepad and pen. "President Moore, what is your opinion on the upcoming school board vote to join the proposed Memorial Tax Incremental Reinvestment Zone, and who it would benefit?"

The questions, Walker desired to tell Miss Henry in a way in which he did not lose face, did not have to be *that* specific. "Well, that is a very specific question . . . Duni—"

"Duna."

"The Memorial Tax Incremental Reinvestment Zone, or TIRZ as we call it, presents the district and the City of Houston with a great chance to reinvest tax money to rebuild poor, blighted areas while increasing the value of property and bringing in business and funding infrastructure projects. It's a win-win for poor areas."

"You're saying Memorial is a poor area, President Moore? The zip code is the richest in the state."

"Now wait just a second, Miss. I didn't say Memorial, as such, was poor. What are you writing? Are you a reporter or something?"

"Dunazade is the editor of the school paper, President Moore, and has a keen interest in following current affairs," Miss Henry said. "She even keeps me on my toes."

"Okay," Walker said, still uneasy with the little girl and her line of questioning. Duna. What kind of name was that? There were no Hispanic faces when Walker was at Jefferson. How about some soft-pitch questions? "Frankly, I'm not an expert on the TIRZ. The City of Houston is in charge of it and has already approved it and is only waiting on the school district to approve it to go ahead with it. My good friend City Councilman Skip Brammer is the real expert on it, the one you want to talk to. He can tell you all about how it is essentially a redistribution of taxes. Mayor Whiting and Superintendent Marshall are behind it as well."

"My original question was regarding who it would benefit," Duna said, holding her pen to her notepad.

"The school district. Memorial Independent School District."

"But my family lives on the other side of the Interstate-10 tracks in Spring Branch, also part of MISD but not the Memorial part. The poor part. I am of voting age, and I don't understand why I would vote for someone who supports redistributing taxes that would probably only benefit the commercial real estate companies on the Memorial side."

"First off, your area of Spring Branch, little girl, would probably benefit more by all the infrastructure improvements that will come out of the TIRZ, drawing in businesses to build there that normally wouldn't. This is primarily done by freezing the tax value of the property at the current rate. Secondly, this is a complex issue, with very complicated economics, my dear."

"Economics like the eight million dollars Synergy donated that all went to build the auditorium at Jefferson?" a familiar voice not accompanied by a raised hand asked Walker. With his hat over his heart, Tucker stood and bowed to Duna. "What about the other kids of this school district of ours? The little folks of Spring Branch out at Northcreek High School and Spring Valley High School? I don't know anything about this tax zone, President Moore, but it sounds like moneychangers cutting out the people again. This ain't Huey Long's notion of redistributing taxes to share the wealth. It took a fight like none other, but the Kingfish whipped John D. Rockefeller and the Standard Oil Company moneychangers and their special tax zones when they were buying and selling off Louisiana—"

"Please raise your hand, class, if you wish to ask President Moore a question," Miss Henry said. "The Louisiana Populism movement and Huey Long have nothing to do with the school board."

"Maybe it ought to," Tucker said.

Walker avoided looking directly at the swirling bird's nest atop the bronze monkey suit. Somewhere between the uncontrolled hair and the suit, reptilian eyes protruded and rallied souls.

"Like Duna, I'm concerned. I spoke this morning with some little folks in this district of ours at Memorial Elementary School," Tucker said, still standing in the middle of the class. "And the return of Louisiana's Kingfish might be just the Texas medicine we need."

"The auditorium," Walker said, "was a donation specifically to Jefferson High School after the Jefferson PTA approached Synergy about making a donation in my honor since I am an alumnus here and you needed a new auditorium. We are also helping to build the new ballpark downtown. It is with great pride that I can tell you that we at Synergy are the leading corporate donor in Houston."

Election Day bell signaled time for students to go to their homeroom classes and vote; underclassmen for student council candidates, seniors for class awards.

"Let us thank President Moore for his time," Miss Henry said. "If anyone else is further interested, he or she may ask questions or sit in on school board meetings open to the public the second Monday of every month at the administration building."

"Thank you for having me and challenging me on the issues facing us. Good luck Mustang baseball," Walker said. "It looks like this year could be the year for a run in the playoffs. I hope to see everyone again tonight at Senior Awards Night."

— - — - —

In the Jefferson High School principal's office, Dr. Green, a slim, choppy-haired blonde, flipped through a stack of pink carbon copy detention slips piled on top of her desk. Outside the door, the hum of Mrs. Bryce running final copies for the next day settled over stale afternoon air, the end of the work near, a soothing time the school principal treasured each day alone in her office. Almost illegible handwriting in the upper right hand corner of the crumpled detention form punctured Dr. Green's happiness:

> *I can vouch he's a good kid. Although the reason on this form says he's a bit of a rambler, you wouldn't be a gambler to waive this infraction. He's a drifter all right between bells, I reckon. But in a tight spot, there ain't a teacher in this school who would bet against him being on time.*
>
> *President of the Class of 1999,*
> *Tuck Davis*

"Mrs. Bryce!" Dr. Green yelled through the door after reading eight more scribbled legal suggestions in the stack. "Send for Tucker Davis!"

Dr. Green put her shoes and earrings back on. She opened the bottom drawer of her desk and lifted the senior class file, the weight of an ancient tome, with both hands. She finished her water with two aspirin and reviewed the notes from last week's meeting with Tucker. The file was a case study that three academic degrees and twenty-two years in the field as a teacher, counselor, administrator, and head principal had not prepared Dr. Green for. Teaching and testing standards, budgets and deadlines, and placating meddling rich parents were one thing. Dr. Green heard the rising volume in the front office as Tucker joked and shook every hand. Without water, she ingested two more aspirin and drove her heels into the carpet.

"I like your suit."

"Sit, Tucker," Dr. Green said. She did not want to prolong the meeting by returning the compliment. His suits all had stories. "How is prom going? Did you get price quotes for valet services?"

"I did. Signed with Lagniappe Valet Parking. It was the only Cajun-owned valet service in Houston. Run by an old, easy-going Cajun named J.D. Thibodaux from the same Louisiana hometown as my mother. According to my mom, *lagniappe* means 'a little something extra' in French."

"You *signed* with them?" Dr. Green asked. Quoting was not signing, in Cajun or in English. "How much are they?"

"I haggled until Mr. Thibodaux said he would give us a three-hundred-dollar discount if Jefferson used them again for prom next year. Talked him down to two thousand for the night. And he offered me and ten of my buddies valet positions."

"Two thousand dollars! You talked him into what? Taking the whole prom budget? Lagniappe Valet Parking is a little something extra."

"According to Mr. Thibodaux, that's why they're the best."

Dr. Green squeezed her temples and used her hands to lift her head. The calendar on the wall under the Picasso black and white Don Quixote print read Monday, April 5th. A month more of Tucker. "I want you and the class to start thinking about what the class legacy should be. Perhaps appoint Elliott Taylor to oversee it since he is the class vice president and very good with numbers. Traditionally, it is a gift given by the graduating class to the school with leftover class money. Like a bench or a tile mosaic."

"Class legacy," Tucker said. He leaned back in the chair, lifting the two front legs off the ground. "I didn't know we got to leave one."

"Every class leaves a legacy," Dr. Green said, indicating with her finger for Tucker to return all four legs of the chair to the floor.

"Not like this class, they don't," Tucker said, slamming the chair back down. "This is a historic class, the Class of '99." He stood up and walked over and pointed out the window. "We can't leave another bench or a mosaic, Dr. Green. It needs to be something extra. We need to leave a lasting mark on history. We need to leave a legacy!"

"This is assuming that there is any money left in the class account for the class legacy after our good Cajun friend Mr. Thibodaux gave us such a discounted rate. I will be sure to print him out a certificate of appreciation from Jefferson High School for his graft."

"I think a little something extra like that would mean a lot to him, Dr. Green. He's the kind of guy—"

"Enough about his character. Tonight is Senior Awards Night. Although against my better judgment, I thought, as senior class president you could present the Most Outstanding Teacher and Student Awards."

"You know I'm good for it, Doc."

"Doctor Green," she corrected. "Give the legacy some thought. It doesn't have to be a bench or a tile mosaic, but the class needs to have a legacy."

"This class will have a legacy," Tucker said, "even if I have to give it one. Because there are kids in this class as good and tough as any this school has ever seen. Chock full of fight."

Dr. Green regretted her decision to allow Tucker to

be a presenter as he crawfished out of her office with the grin of a deal having been struck, instead of in full retreat and shame over bestowing his own class the legacy of being several thousand dollars in the red.

— - — - —

Fisher K. Hughes slouched in a navy blazer and tried to shake his dead skin twenty rows behind the last row of parents and students in the Walker B. Moore Auditorium. The dead skin fell from his thick hair, still a boyish brown with the odd gray hair. Fisher swept the downfall of sticky dandruff with his hands off his shoulders and into his lap. Open next to his audio recorder, an unreturned library copy of *The Magic Christian* he brought for the assignment collected the dead skin in his lap. He was certain he did not want any of his ashes spread in the Walker B. Moore Auditorium.

Fisher undid the top button constraining his collar. The bottom of his Paisley tie was thrown over his right shoulder and hung around his neck like a noose. He refolded the pastel yellow handkerchief a former boyfriend had given him for his birthday and seated it in the front breast pocket of his blazer. The recorder in his lap capturing Walker's speech, Fisher concentrated on tuning out the voice of his classmate from the Jefferson High School Class of 1964 who he had come to interview about the new auditorium.

"I haven't forgotten that first day of work after graduating from Harvard Business School. My dad always told me growing up, 'To know oil and gas, son, you got to get your hands dirty. The roughnecks won't ever respect you until you share the same risks they take.' He was right," Walker said, his fit fifty-three-year-old body still setting his head in the posture taught in manners class. "Not that I was a stranger to risk. I had served as a pilot in the Texas Air National Guard during the Vietnam era. But it was nothing like that first summer day I spent in the oil fields of West Texas when we had to rope a flailing busted pipe."

At least the old auditorium's poor acoustics kept an old bore like Walker Moore from ruining a good read. Sharing risks and roughing it? Fisher had been to Vietnam, volunteering to extend for a second combat tour as a Marine in the southern delta while Walker patrolled unforgiving business school classrooms. It must take an auditorium with enhanced sound transmission and your name on it, Fisher snorted to himself.

"We hope the relationship between Memorial Independent School District and Synergy will continue to blossom, and it is my privilege to represent both of them on this day. Congratulations again to all the students we honored earlier tonight with awards for their achievements. Let me finish by saying that, although the sun may have set on the great oil boom glory days of the early nineteen-eighties—when many of you were born—we at Synergy believe we carry on the great Houston tradition of wildcatting. We think of ourselves as both the last of the wildcatters of the twentieth-century and the first of the innovators of the twenty-first century. Thank you, and as president of the school board I officially open your new Jefferson High School Walker B. Moore Auditorium." Last Wildcatter Hits Dry Hole with Audience at Alma Mater, the working title of Fisher's article, was ruined by the standing ovation Walker received as he returned to his seat in the first row.

A skinny boy in an oversized, old-fashioned suit rose from the chair onstage beside the school principal. He ambled over to the podium as if he had been riding horses his whole life and introduced himself as Jefferson High School Senior Class President Tucker Davis. He held a fedora hat, and not a speech, in his hand. Fisher, the Jefferson High School Senior Class President of 1964, examined Tucker for likeness. He found none.

"I promised Dr. Green I wouldn't come here and talk politics tonight. And I reckon y'all didn't come here to listen to politics either. Y'all came here tonight to get your fair due, what was owed to y'all. But for anyone here tonight who didn't get an award, I say to you, hold that head of yours up and bull straight ahead, because I'll be right there alongside you in the fight."

Fisher looked at his program. Who was Tucker addressing? Aside from Tucker, all the students invited to Senior Awards Night were recipients of at least one award.

"And one person who has been there alongside us in the fight is the Most Outstanding Teacher, even though there ain't anyone tarring us more about our grammar. Your favorite twelfth grade English teacher, that lover of literature, a knight of the round table and seeker of the holy grail, the white whale herself, Mrs. Bridge!"

A pretty-faced, portly lady accepted the plaque. Fisher cheered as Tucker encouraged the crowd to coax her into giving a speech. The Most Outstanding Teacher of the Year returned to her seat reddened and not having uttered a word.

"This next award was voted on by the senior class," Tucker said to the crowd. "The recipient lives the old motto of the Texas Rangers lawmen, 'Little man whip a big man every time if the little man's in the right and keeps a-coming.' Again and again, steaming head-on, making sure the senior class got the whole hog. The whole hog! My best friend and vice president, the first ever four-time Most Outstanding Student Award winner in Jefferson High School history, Elliott "Whole Hog" Taylor!"

Fisher wondered where they had found this madman as Tucker tried to stir the baffled auditorium crowd by chanting into the microphone, "Whole Hog!" Tucker presented the award to a tall, All-American looking blonde kid. Fisher stood up with the crowd and applauded the student who waved and made his way back to his seat with the plaque.

Tucker donned his hat and placed his hands in his front pants pockets.

"I said I wouldn't talk about politics," Tucker said. "Fact right now I'm supposed to be telling y'all about the drinks and refreshments we got set up outside for digging into."

Fisher moved up twenty rows. In front of him onstage, the school principal, who had projected poise as emcee of the ceremony, was squirming in her seat. Tucker removed his hat from his head.

"I didn't come here to talk politics," Tucker said. "Nor did I come here to anoint a king tonight either." He clenched his right fist and leveled it at Walker. "I came here tonight because this is a class with a legacy. The legacy in the courage of a Whole Hog Taylor, of a Persian girl in this audience not afraid to stand up in her American government class and question the school board president about the selling off of our school district into special tax zones. How did I not see this? I, Tuck Catfish Davis, the senior class president, the one y'all trusted and who swore a fight against corruption. How did I not hear it?" His clenched fist opened and his fingers spread as his hand rose above the audience.

"And that ain't the half of it. I want y'all to feast on that whole hog and not just the leg and scraps they throw us when the barbeque is over. 'Four weeks,' they said, 'and Catfish won't have a whisker in anything here anymore.' But hear me now, and y'all tell them Tuck Davis said, 'They ain't bled that stubborn Louisiana Long blood out of Catfish yet.' Catfish went down to his old elementary school and had a talk with some little folks. They said, 'Catfish, your enemies always call you crazed and crooked.' Well, let them paint me crazy, because I've been crazy to let them plunder what's been owed to little folks like y'all."

The brown eyes thrust out, pushed up by gushing words. "It's about time we start doing some stealing from those that have stolen this district from us. With these school board representatives and president," Tucker denounced, "there soon won't be anything left to steal! I want the whole hog and I aim to steal it and give it to the little folks of Memorial Independent School District. Slander me what they will, but us little folks will have a legacy of change and fight."

Parents next to Fisher put their arms around their children. Fisher checked to make sure his audio recorder was on.

"School board," Tucker said. "I filed an hour before the deadline at four o'clock today in the administration building to run for school board seat number five held by sitting President Walker B. Moore. I, Catfish Davis, officially announce my candidacy in the district election for school board. With the blessing of Governors Huey Long, Earl Long, and Bobby Boudreaux, I enter this fight for school board. Every kid a king!"

In his double-breasted suit, a fight vowed on behalf of poor folks—which Fisher was sure included no one in the crowd—Tucker Davis stood onstage, his hands outstretched on each side to the people, with the blessing of two deceased governors and one on trial.

Below the fedora held in the air, Walker held his stomach in the first row. Onstage, a runaway pipe gushed. As Fisher came around the aisle, he saw his old classmate once again locked in a contest with a flailing pipe.

Tucker bent back over the microphone. "Dunazade Shari, will you go to senior prom with me?"

Walker vomited on the recorder thrust in his face for comment by his old classmate Fisher Hughes.

Two

Dear Governor Boudreaux, Tucker wrote at his bedroom desk, sandwiched between towers of political biographies, *From what I can make of reading about the legal proceedings from down here in Houston, it sure sounds like you got them on the run again. Not even them New Orleans newspapermen can say otherwise, though they'd just as soon swap their first-born kid to string up the Cajun King and kick you out of the state mansion for good. Eight grand juries and three indictments later, you're still fighting as the only four-time elected governor of Louisiana. Not even our Uncle Earl Long, Last of the Red Hot Poppas, managed to get either indicted or elected this many times—and he was a Long!*

I wish you and your wife, the beautiful Mrs. Candy Boudreaux, my best. I know you make her proud. Because you make all of us proud out there fighting for the little folks. If you're a crook, well, I'll vote for the crook every time. Who do these folks calling you a crook and testifying against you for racketeering and extortion think gave them their jobs? I hope they call me to testify about this same "crook," and I will tell them a story about a small-town, twelve-year-old kid from Acadia Parish, a young populist called the Cajun King, who believed every kid should be a king, going door to door in the swamps to install electricity for poor folks for free after teaching himself how. If that kid is a crook, I hope all kids in this world are crooked. I've got the troops lined up behind you west of your state border—you just give me the nod and your Gulf Coast brethren will be there. Because nobody treats Governor Bobby Boudreaux this way. I'll dig up and resurrect Huey Long if I have to for the fight.

Tucker paused to look above his desk on the wall at an unsmiling Huey Long. Huey posed with his left hand in his double-breasted suit front pocket next to a car with a United States Senate license plate, ready for a fight with his right hand. Tucker wondered, if the Kingfish had declared to run for school board, would his announcement have been as misunderstood by his classmates as Tucker's was after Senior Awards Night when everyone avoided him at the refreshments table outside. Only Duna seemed to notice, accepting his invite to prom; and Elliott, who gave Tucker a ride home from the awards ceremony while Tucker rode shotgun and held Elliott's fourth consecutive Most Outstanding Student Award plaque in his lap. The only student without an award in hand afterwards at the refreshments table, Tucker took comfort in knowing Huey Long's political stances had not always won him popularity among his classmates and teachers.

"As long as I got your approval, Kingfish, I'm going to keep stumping for little folks until they get honored like they deserve," Tucker said to the black and white photo of Huey Long on his wall and continued his frenetic writing.

I also enclosed for you, Governor Boudreaux, a copy of the article in the paper written about me declaring my candidacy for school board. The seat is held by a representative in his second term who is doubling as the president of the school board. I can take this guy on and lick him good. He does have wealth and the establishment behind him and many powerful rainmaker friends in the district, so it won't be easy competing against him. What he doesn't have is a pint of Long blood in him. Nor the Cajun vote, which between you, J.D. Thibodaux of Lagniappe Valet Parking, and me, we can pretty much guarantee.

Although I have yet to really start raising money, the little cash I have raised so far has been promising. If you have any advice about school board elections, I would be glad to hear it. Don't you worry about a damn thing sitting in that courtroom listening to that prosecutor spin yarns about you and the way you do business for the little folks. They have accused you, Huey, Earl, and me all before, and we're all still standing, just itching for another fight on behalf of little folks. You turn the horns of the bull on them.

Every Kid a King,
Tuck Catfish Davis
School Board Seat Number Five Candidate

Finished, Tucker placed his unfinished math homework in his senior yearbook. Now that he was a candidate running for office again, Tucker hoped he could get some of his classmates' signatures in his yearbook. In his junior-year yearbook Tucker kept a photocopy of the nearly four hundred signatures he collected from his class in petitioning to end the water monopoly. Tucker never forgot his parents' faces when he came home from school and showed them the list and the number of friends he had. Not a lot of people signed his yearbook, but the collection of almost four hundred signatures was something no other classmate could brag about.

Tucker picked out a wrinkled navy blue tie with pink polka dots from a pile of ties on the floor of his closet. A green and white computer test form from his history class stuck out underneath the pile. At the top of the test circled in red was a score of sixty-eight. Tucker stuffed the test in his pocket so his parents did not discover it. His argument about the overrated value of grades was not helped by the fact that Elliott weighed Harvard and Princeton acceptance offers after four years of straight A's. It was a cause of great frustration to Tucker that parents were often unaware that Huey Long received bad grades in high school and had gotten into trouble with his teachers as well. Huey's brother Earl, Tucker reassured himself calmly, achieved such bad progress reports in high school that he skipped college for the office of governor. Still, Tucker wondered if he made a mistake in only applying to one university, a top private university in Louisiana the college counselor warned Tucker had come a long way academically since the days when Huey Long studied law there for a semester.

"We're going to do this, Kingfish," Tucker said to Huey Long, as he tightened his tie in the mirror next to his desk. "To make history, you got to know history and be able to rouse it. It ain't going to be easy, and it will take every strong-arm tactic you perfected."

"Tucker," Mrs. Davis called from the kitchen, "your breakfast is ready."

Tucker grabbed his senior yearbook and folded the newspaper article inside the letter as he went into the kitchen.

"Don't you look nice in your uncle's old suit," Mrs. Davis said to Tucker. Like her son, Mrs. Davis had a mass of chestnut curls atop a smile that stretched across her face.

"Like a prohibition gangster," Dr. Davis said, looking up from the *Chronicle* at his son dressed in a cream-colored, double-breasted suit and tan fedora. Several inches shorter than Tucker and with neatly combed dark hair and a rabbinical demeanor, Dr. Davis was more often mistaken for an uncle when standing next to his son. "Or like one of those Louisianan politicians of yours. Same class of criminal actually."

Tucker put the letter on the table. "Can you express mail this for me today?"

"Sure," Mrs. Davis said. She held up her stained purple

hands and smiled. "Now eat your fresh blackberries that I picked for your pancakes." Mrs. Davis picked buckets of blackberries from an uncut church ditch across town in the Third Ward, leaving her fingers stained for days afterwards.

"Why do you write letters to this rogue who never writes you back?" Dr. Davis asked. "I ask you, if a tree falls in the forest and no one is around to hear it, does it make a sound?"

"My letter wishes Governor Boudreaux well against the ridiculous charges of corruption that have been falsely imposed upon him by another politically-motivated prosecutor."

"Why does the city section look as if a team of armadillos charged onto a football field through it?" Dr. Davis asked holding up the gored section of the paper.

"I think it's very nice of you to send him a letter, Tucker. Everyone in this country is innocent until proven guilty," Mrs. Davis said to Dr. Davis who rolled his eyes through the giant hole in the paper.

"My letter also contains the article I cut out of the city section earlier this morning about declaring my candidacy for school board last night at Senior Awards Night."

"You declared *what* last night?" Dr. Davis asked.

"I am a candidate for position number five on the Memorial Independent School District school board."

"You're an eighteen-year-old kid," Dr. Davis said. "You can't be an official candidate for school board. You can't even legally consume alcohol in this country for another three years. How is it even theoretically possible for you to go into politics?"

Tucker unfolded the letter and handed him the *Chronicle* article. "They made the same claims when I ran for senior class president. This time I aim to steal back this district of ours that Walker Moore and his cronies have taken."

"'They' who?" Dr. Davis put down his coffee and read

the article. "You can't feasibly run against your old baseball coach. How is the *Chronicle* interested in you? Is this one of your attempts at that peculiar strand of humor of yours?"

"School board," Mrs. Davis said reading the headline. "That's great, Tucker. If only your Uncle Remy were still alive, he would be so proud of you going into district politics. You're even campaigning in one of his old suits and hat."

"Yes," Dr. Davis said, "crazy coonass Uncle Remy would be most proud. That's precisely who we want our son to aspire to. A flamboyant character in one of your Uncle Remy's lies about the carnival of Louisiana politics."

"I asked Dunazade Shari to the prom last night."

"That's great, Tucker," Mrs. Davis said. "She's the editor of the school paper, right?"

Elliott's truck pulled up in the driveway. Tucker grabbed his yearbook and fedora.

"Definitely don't forget your thinking hat," Dr. Davis yelled at Tucker, who scampered out the front door. "That will get you into college. According to our beloved Uncle Remy, that was once Earl Long's hat before it became our family heirloom."

"It's probably just a phase, dear," Mrs. Davis said.

"That's what we said ten years ago when he first started showing these symptoms after listening to your Uncle Remy's absurd Louisiana political folklore and stories. Do you not remember how Walker Moore couldn't get Tucker to practice baseball because he was so busy practicing his speeches to his teammates, then rallying them at games when they were already leading their opponent by ten runs? Not that there is a God, but couldn't he have blessed us with a halfway normal teenager for our only child? I don't doubt that fedora of Tucker's is the same hat Earl Long wore when he lost his sanity and they confined him to the mental institution. The Cursed Fedora theory of mine would at least explain some of this madness."

"Tucker needs something to balance out his poor grades and not being the most popular kid in school," Mrs. Davis said, scrubbing Tucker's plate in the sink. "Most parents would be happy their son is running for office and wants to serve. He likes to help people."

"Our errant holy fool needs to help himself," Dr. Davis said as he cut his pancakes into four even sections.

"Try to be philosophical about this."

"Because I'm a philosophy professor? Our son subscribes to a philosophy professed by scheming corrupt demagogues in the most toxic backwater state in the country!"

"Good enough state for your wife and her family!" Mrs. Davis snatched her husband's plate holding the stack of pancakes he was eating, leaving him only the one pancake section on his fork. "You confuse colorful characters with corruption."

"I love you, dear, but it's a banana republic down there in Louisiana. Take Bobby Boudreaux as a case in point. He's a governor and about to be sent to prison!"

"He can't be all that bad or he wouldn't have been elected governor four times and be a hero to our son. Our son is running for school board, and no position demands more ethics. Tucker would have to be crazy to write Bobby Boudreaux if he were as awful as everything they write about him."

"Precisely! Therein lies my point."

— - — - —

"School board?"

"School board," Fisher echoed the editor. Fisher perched on one of the indestructible steel chairs in the editor's office that management refused to replace.

"I don't buy it," the editor said. "You're a born cynic, Hughes."

"Not by nature."

"STUDENT UPSTAGES PRESIDENT AT SYNERGY AUDITORIUM DEDICATION BY DECLARING CANDIDACY," the editor read the headline aloud. "I can't get over that I let you print this. You work twenty years at one paper and you get a bone thrown your way occasionally. Isn't this Synergy executive your old classmate, Hughes? You sure you don't have an axe to grind? Those boys at Synergy don't play very nice, and they don't like to be portrayed in print as anything but the brightest minds out there. This city is a goddamn small town."

"I don't have anything personal against Walker Moore. I've known Walker since we were little, though I would never have thought he would be the one to go into politics. In fact, Walker was my first boyhood crush."

"Would you spare me your first homosexual encounters, Hughes? It is uncomfortable enough tolerating your bewildering personality without factoring in your homosexuality."

"You're telling me, chief," Fisher said. "Try being gay for twenty-four hours. Or being a gay Marine." Fisher tried to recall his days as a Marine. But the built-in skepticism he credited to having been a grunt in Vietnam dismissed the blurry image of himself in fatigues after a moment. It was getting harder to sniff out the bullshit.

"I'm not seeing the political significance of this race," the editor said.

"The rumor is that after this school board race, Walker Moore plans to run for Congress when Bill Archibald announces his expected retirement later this year. Walker might be the favorite, or even go unchallenged because of the wealthy pockets he could tap into."

"And you think this story about a kid running for school board has legs? The kid sounds crazy to me."

"My rule of thumb is the smaller the politics, the uglier

the politics. The kid calls himself Catfish for Christ's sake. He believes he is the long lost descendant of Huey Long and Earl Long and that his legacy is to fight for the little folks out there. Legs? It's got fins to swim, chief. I know it. You can't even make this up about his heroes being the Longs."

"He has to be crazy if the Longs are his political heroes."

"He's a kid," Fisher said. "How does he even know who those guys are? He told me an anecdote after the awards night about a high school Huey Long campaigning successfully to get his own principal fired after being expelled." Fisher scratched his itchy head and smiled. "You should have seen this kid onstage. Even after the ceremony, none of the parents knew what was going on. He was shaking hands and tossing off quotes to me and anyone else who would listen. He told me to note that he won't be accepting any soft money."

"Soft money?"

"Large donations usually given by big businesses and individuals to a party organization or political action committee who indirectly—"

"I know damn well what it is. Individuals can't accept soft money, and it's a school board election anyway, Hughes. How much money is even out there from corporations?"

"I wouldn't think that much. Who knows and who cares?" Fisher came around to the other side of the editor's desk. "This kid could be the human interest story of the decade in this town." Fisher framed a picture with his hands a foot away from the editor's face and narrated, "HOUSTON KID RUNS FOR AMERICAN DREAM—DEFENDS DISTRICT, FIGHTS FOR HAVE-NOTS, THE PEOPLE'S POPULIST, SCHOOL BOARD SAVIOR."

"Sure, Pulitzer," the editor said, waving away Fisher's hands. "You can do one more on this kid. I suppose we can never get enough human interest coverage of our eccentrics in this city. People do love populists."

"That's why they're populists," Fisher said, half-way out the door.

The city flattened out as Fisher escaped through the glass maze of downtown. He rolled down the windows of his car to let the weedy discharge of the bayou ride with him west along Allen Parkway. The moist breeze attached to Fisher's skin at stoplights. The drive west always began with all possibilities on the table as Fisher journeyed through the pine forest of Memorial Park to the Memorial Villages west of the I-610 Loop. Yesterday his old school, today a catfish. Fisher spread the possibilities for tomorrow out in his mind.

White-bricked and dome-roofed Jefferson High School was nestled away at the end of the Villages, where the egg buildings had sat for almost forty years undisturbed. The main office Fisher walked into was well-lit. Women typed at keyboards and chatted in cubicles. Others darted in and out of openings in the walls. Fisher approached a tall, plump woman typing behind a desk at the end of the office. "I was wondering where I could find the school principal."

"Dr. Green is sick today."

Induced by Senior Awards Night, Fisher diagnosed. "I'm a reporter for the *Chronicle*. I was hoping I could speak to her." Fisher handed the woman a business card. She set it beside a half-eaten sandwich on her desk. "Do you and the students no longer get a designated lunch break?"

"Usually we just eat at our desks because it gets so busy. But the students still get about an hour every day until noon."

Long glass windows, interrupted only by doors, surrounded all four sides of the Jefferson High School cafeteria. Attached to the cafeteria was a wooden deck where a few groups of students played cards and ate their lunches. Inside the fish bowl cafeteria, Fisher easily spotted the catfish he sought against the wall next to a small school desk. A poster taped to the desk advertised talent show tickets for sale. In a cream-colored, double-breasted suit, Tucker appeared to be lecturing a pretty girl who dug through her bag. Could she be the prom date? A tall, handsome boy behind the desk took notes. Fisher recognized the boy as the Most Outstanding Student Award recipient from the night before.

"You're going to need to open a bank account for campaign donations," Tucker said to the boy behind the table. Tucker addressed the girl, "The profile coming out on the front page of *The Pony Express* is a good start, Duna, but we're going to need continuous coverage. This is our mouthpiece to attack Walker Moore. I need y'all to start digging. Research his decisions as president of the school board. Find something we can chew on. Put your best reporter on it, preferably you. You were all over him yesterday about the zoning thing. When does the paper come out?"

"Thursday morning, after third period," Duna said, walking out the door with her bag.

"Good. We will campaign on Thursday at lunch, Elliott," Tucker said to the boy behind the desk, "and strike while we have this bull by the horns. Why, Mr. Hughes, if it ain't great to see you." Tucker smiled and stepped forward to shake hands with Fisher. Tucker turned back to Elliott but kept his grip on Fisher's hand and asked Elliott, "What about Friday?"

"Friday is the class field trip to the zoo."

"Which is free transportation outside the campaign budget to press the flesh with some voters. I like it. Mr. Hughes, have you met my best friend and campaign manager, Vice President Elliott Taylor?"

"Elliott Whole Hog Taylor, right?" Fisher joked. Elliott shrugged. Fisher shook Elliott's hand and interpreted Elliott's shrug to mean that the title originated with Tucker. Fisher could not conceive what force had fused together this odd pairing.

"As you can see, Mr. Hughes, we are hashing out a

strategy to defeat Walker Moore," Tucker said. "A strategy is needed to take down this district-size giant squid and cut off his tentacles."

"Can I quote you on that?" Fisher asked, kicking himself for not insisting on a photographer for the assignment. Fisher got the sense that it was normal in Tucker's world for a class president to wear a double-breasted suit.

"I want you to put it in bold print, all capital letters. Next to, 'Tentacles don't work on Tuck Davis' leather hide!' Ask anyone here at Jefferson about my toughness." Tucker stomped the cafeteria floor with his black and white two-toned shoes. "My poor mom gave birth to an alligator."

"I thought you were a fish."

"Catfish is hopping mad at what old Walker Moore has done to this district. There ain't classification for such a thing," Tucker clarified. "Call me a bull moose with wings if you want to in your paper, as long as I'm against Walker Moore and fighting for the people of this district."

"How is your campaign going so far today?"

"On Day One, already better than Walker Moore's entire reelection campaign to date. Every kid a king, but no one man wears a crown! Look out at them." Tucker gestured to the long white tables of students in the cafeteria smelling of pizza, the chatter at the tables one loud cafeteria conversation. "All they want is a damn chance. There are four hundred sixty-two seniors at Jefferson High School, four hundred or so are eighteen. I'm going to get all those votes."

"Takes more than four hundred votes to win a school board election."

"How many votes did it take in the last election to win?" Tucker asked Elliott.

"Last year school board seat number four incumbent Watkins beat Landers one thousand eight hundred to one thousand two hundred," Elliott said, flipping a sheet of paper. "Three years ago, Moore drummed Elkins, capturing precisely two thousand three hundred sixty-one to nine hundred fifty-three votes. You remember Robert Elkins from middle school, Tuck? After Mr. Elkins' school board election defeat, he started home-schooling Robert and his younger brother—"

"We'll get over three thousand votes," Tucker said. "With five high schools in the district, that alone is a little over three thousand seniors' votes right there. That's my base."

"Not the most reliable voting demographic, teenagers about to graduate," Fisher reminded Tucker, who seemed to be even less grounded in mathematics than in reality.

"This ain't a traditional campaign either. I suppose you came looking for an interview, Mr. Hughes. Let me start by showing you my base."

Fisher remembered hating lunch, that great divider, the forty-five minutes in high school separating factions, sitting with the boys but secretly never one of them. He followed Tucker to the first table over, a table of pretty girls all dressed in designer outfits Fisher guessed cost more than his weekly salary. At the far end of the table, a mother in workout clothes and her daughter ate the restaurant salads the mother had brought to school.

"Ladies, ladies," Tucker said. He held his hat with both hands at his chest. The girls at the table giggled. "I probably should not bother y'all, but I take it y'all have heard by this time about my candidacy for school board."

"You're running against Walker," the prettiest girl asserted.

"President Moore," Tucker said, "seat number—"

"Five," a blonde boy in a letter jacket walking up said. The boy leaned over and kissed the girl who had been talking to Tucker. A group of five other male students of equally impressive physical stature loitered behind the boy. "My father's position."

"That's right, Chuck. I understand if you and the missus here have to vote for your old man. Sometimes you got to dance with them that brought you."

"You know why they call him Catfish?" Chuck Moore asked Fisher. "Because he's a bottom feeder, our class clown." The table of girls and group behind Chuck laughed.

"Like senior class president," Tucker said, "I won the vote for class clown."

"You won that race in a landslide, Catfish. There's no funnier joke than you in our class," Chuck said. He laughed and walked away holding hands with the girl.

"This bottom feeder might have to expand his base to scavenge the necessary votes," Tucker said to Fisher, who was wondering if Tucker even had a base. It certainly was not the cool kids, Fisher noted.

Tucker asked for the support of the students at the next table over. The students told Tucker they would vote for their classmate, but insisted that Tucker pledge to abolish all homework and change the lunch selection in the cafeteria to pizza every day.

"I'm just the kid to do it, y'all," Tucker said. "Who ended water's monopoly and got y'all a Dr Pepper machine in here just like he said he'd do?"

"Catfish did."

"Someone's got to look after your health around here, and it ain't Walker Moore. This time I need not only your signatures on a petition, but also your votes at the ballot box."

The two lone black students in the Jefferson High School cafeteria sat at the end of the next table over. Tucker explained to Fisher that the Curry twins, like his friend Duna, were picked up by a special bus on the north side of the interstate and brought to school each day. Fisher nodded and trailed behind Tucker, who promised him an interview after this last crucial campaign stop. Fisher calculated the total of likely voters for Tucker to be still at zero.

"If Catfish can't count on the Curry boys to deliver, then I don't know what I'm doing in this race."

"Catfish," the twins said in unison.

"Gentlemen, I'm calling in a favor."

"Catfish needs the African-American vote it sounds like," Kingsley Curry said.

"All two of us," Edwin Curry said.

"Two going on two thousand. I have to know the Curry boys are behind me and not Walker Moore. Like Uncle Earl Long before me, they will have to call me crazy and put me in the nuthouse before I turn my back on the blacks. Us little folks got to stick together."

"You are one of the little folks like us, Tucker, because your father is Jewish?" Edwin asked.

"Not the same, old boy, hardly a minority at all," Kingsley said. "Catfish's mother is Cajun, though. There has been some documented discrimination of Cajuns in Texas."

"We're doing pretty well actually, even if like you, Tucker, we have no shot at being a member of the country club," Edwin said. "We both got accepted to Rice this week."

"Congratulations," Tucker said slapping them on their backs. "That is quite the university. You know my pappy does a bit of teaching there."

"Pappy. How does he have a *pappy*?" Edwin turned and asked Fisher. "Your father's a professor with a doctorate in philosophy, Tuck."

"And a Jew," Kingsley said. "*Pappy* really is the antithesis of 'father' in Yiddish. The name Davis could pass for a black name though, brother."

"This is true," Edwin said.

Tucker shook Edwin's Dr Pepper to see if there was any left. "I'm going to have to give him fair warning all the same that trouble in the name of the Curry Gang is riding through there."

Edwin seized his Dr Pepper from Tucker. "Count the

Curry Gang in, Tuck. Why not one last adventure with our brother, Catfish Davis? We did make up the African-American contingent last year, an instrumental block in the great Share Our Wealth Coalition."

"Why not indeed, good brother," Kingsley said. "A voice in politics is not to be laughed at."

"Not the voice of the people," Tucker seconded.

"Give them hell, Tuck!" Kingsley cheered.

"I aim to send them there."

"What do you two assess Tucker's chances are of defeating President Moore in the school board election?" Fisher asked.

"I'm a believer," Edwin said, "but not good. Parents are going to find it difficult voting for an eighteen-year-old student. With a name like Catfish Davis, they're going to think they're voting for an old knuckleballer Negro League pitcher turned ward political boss."

"*Not good*," Kingsley said, "is all the odds Catfish Davis ever needed. He's got the Jefferson black vote wrapped up, and he represents more than just the Memorial good-old-boy interests. If it takes a crazy fool to even run for office, there certainly can't be any candidates out there crazier than Catfish."

"There ain't," Tucker said. "I'm stir-crazy. When the rest of them candidates are sleeping, I'm politicking."

— - — - —

Dr. Green never could believe how much art per square block filled the Neartown area of Houston. Born a military brat, Dr. Green's Houston neighborhood was a long way from the military bases where the annually painted rocks were displayed. When Dr. Green bought her blue and yellow bungalow in the early nineteen-eighties before the oil industry crashed in Texas, her neighbors were all artists getting by on government grants and an occasional sold work. After a day at work, she would hurry home for a jog as many of them began their day, and join them for a drink in the evening on their porch swings, the shiny sluggish night sky coming down on them, slowly sucking their cotton clothes through the tiny gaps between the wooden slats of the swings.

Marrying one of the artists, Dr. Green later learned, was not as easy as listening to their entertaining accounts over cocktails. But she remained loyal to the street of nineteen-thirties bungalows long after her short marriage ended, and long after the neighborhood began to be consumed from the inside by a tidal wave of ugly, three-story townhomes sprouting up as fast as the developers could tear down the bungalows and build a profit. Dr. Green parked in front of one of these townhomes, a gaudy stone three-story affair higher than any other house on the street, whose new owner now only had a ten-minute drive to downtown.

Two blocks to the south was the famed Menil Collection, but three blocks to the north was a closing art gallery Dr. Green desired to visit first. There was no way to stop the tide of these townhomes. A cycle of the new, the townhomes drove up prices until an owner could not afford not to sell. It was Houston. Progress over preservation, Darwinism played out in buildings, no association to mediate in the boomtown of boomtowns.

Because there were no sidewalks, Dr. Green strolled in the narrow street exploring the character of each house and noting the state of its banana trees, playing hooky from school at forty-six years of age. Dr. Green wondered what would be the legacy of the closing gallery. A new two-story townhome, or a new three-story townhome? A sign of the times, there was no mention in the paper about its closing. But there was an article on Tucker Davis, several paragraphs on his legacy. School board. Dr. Green feared she had planted this legacy in his unhinged mind in her office. A notice on the art gallery door declared the gallery closed, the paintings all sold. The one painting remaining was on the small lawn. On a wooden sign, the painting was of the future two-story modern townhome to be built on the site. "If new is king here," Dr. Green said to her adopted city, rapping the wooden painting with her fist, "then at least Tucker Davis will be old."

— - — - —

"Who drives you to do this?" Walker asked the red 1965 Mustang convertible occupying his reserved Synergy parking space. "That's twice this week you've stolen my space when I went to pick up my dry cleaning." Walker parked next door at Antioch Missionary Baptist Church. The stone steeple and its message in black—JESUS SAVES—was at the foot of the Synergy north tower. A dazzling reflection of all light, the new Synergy north tower connected to the other glass-scaled south tower on Smith Street by a new enclosed circular skywalk on the fourth floor over the street traffic. At night, the white crown at the top of each tower was lit along with the skywalk, a glowing downtown space battleship.

Outside the front entrance at 1400 Smith Street stood the Synergy logo, a five-foot thick, clear glass letter S the height of Walker, tilted to lean at a forty-five degree angle. The Slithering S, his friend Skip Brammer called the logo. Walker and his dry cleaning passed through security into a museum of modern art and sculptures. The wife of the chief operations officer added a new piece of art each week to the lobby. A recorded voice from the flat screen television in the elevator insisted Walker consider for thirty-eight floors whether he rode every day on the edge of the cutting edge of adventurous solutions. Reaching the executive offices on the thirty-ninth floor, the voice informed Walker he was at the edge.

The office of Synergy Capital & Trade President Walker B. Moore was at the end of the thirty-ninth floor, across from the office of the chief operations officer. Walker's attractive secretary told him that Fisher Hughes was waiting in his tiny, two hundred square-foot office.

After Synergy was named Most Innovative Company by the leading business biweekly for the fifth straight year in 1998, Walker was given the option of moving to a larger office. Walker declined; his office felt like home. The Synergy CEO—whose folksy patriarchal demeanor balanced the naked ruthlessness and competitiveness of the much younger chief operations officer to create the company culture—declined to move offices as well. Instead, the CEO tore down two of his office walls to get the feel of his new office "just right."

"I value vision and ideas and trade them like oil and gas," the CEO had said to Walker and others gathered to watch the CEO ceremoniously swing the sledgehammer into the office wall. "How can you expect me to work in an office with walls?" the CEO later asked Walker. Mystified he himself had not seen the genius in this novel managing concept of eliminating limits in the workplace, Walker did not argue that the CEO still had walls in his office, or that eliminating the old ones forced two of their colleagues to relocate. Sense of home in an office be damned, Walker could not wait for the next opportunity to move offices and tear down a wall and keep a sledgehammer by his desk afterwards like the CEO.

Fisher was standing by the cabinet and reading the inscriptions on the deal toys displayed in Walker's office. Walker said to Fisher, who held a glass statue of a man in Arab dress on a camel, "That figure is meant to be Lawrence of Arabia. We really swooped in there on a pipeline deal to the

Arabian Sea through one of those unpronounceable Arabic villages."

"Walker B. Moore, the Last Wildcatter," Fisher said.

"Walker B. Moore, the Last Wildcatter," Walker repeated the new title. "Closer of deals, driller of wells. I'm going to see if my colleagues will start referring to me by that around the office. I should be able to make my subordinates call me that."

"I take it business is bustling these days?"

"Our stock keeps going up. Got the annual Synergy International Conference kickoff meeting tonight," Walker said, rocking back in his chair. "This year I am resolved that my team will win the prize for the funniest skit. I have hired University of Houston theatre professors to give my Synergy Capital & Trade team acting lessons and make us funny."

"What do you think about your opponent? His age? And the criticisms he is leveling against you?"

"I happen to know the kid in question as I was once his coach," Walker said, declining to mention that Tucker had been the only kid he had ever coached who did not call him "coach." "I have little doubt that he means well. He will learn a lot of positive things from this experiment in our democratic process."

Fisher flipped to the back of his notepad. "How do you respond to his statements earlier today, and I quote, 'Walker Moore is a moneychanger who has kept the whole hog for himself,' 'The worst president since Warren G. Harding,' and 'The heir to Judas, who at least had the political decency to only ask for thirty pieces of silver'? He also said in reference to your abortive nineteen eighty-eight state senate run, 'Walker Moore has a whole lot of quit in him. You quit once in politics, you quit twice. Catfish Davis has more fight in the marrow of one whisker than the quitter Walker Moore's got blood in him. Strip him of his throne, and every kid is a king.'"

"Tucker said what?" Walker rose from his chair. *Quit once, quit twice* was Walker's own line; one intended for sports and not the game of life. Why was life assailing him from all angles this week? While Fisher was scribbling in his notepad, Walker wondered if this all could have been avoided if he had placed Tucker in some spot other than last in the batting order that season. "He's never run anything in his life. Declaring is the easy part, Fisher. I've heard no new ideas or policies in these statements, just bombs being thrown."

Fisher turned a page in his notepad. "Tucker Davis also announced that he will 'not accept any money from the corporations feeding at the trough with Walker Moore.'"

"I will not even deem such mudslinging worthy of a response. I am entirely transparent, as are the dealings of the school district board of trustees. We are the best school district in the state. It is no small distinction for me to preside over the school district as president, carrying on in the same great tradition as when we were there and led the way, Fisher."

"I don't seem to recall you having a big place in student government back then, Walker."

"I wasn't as active as you, Senior Class President Hughes. I used to think you would be Senator Hughes or even President of the United States one day. When are you running?"

"Me?" Fisher laughed. "My interest in politics is fulfilled by covering politics. I have too many liabilities to be a candidate. I didn't check enough of the boxes in life after college."

"But you were the most well-liked guy in our class. You were a Marine in Vietnam."

"That's about the only box I checked. Not sure what I proved by that either." Fisher stood up. "I appreciate your time, Walker. It was nice catching up. Sorry if I held you here a little past closing time."

"Anytime, classmate," Walker said, escorting Fisher out.

"Remember to vote in three weeks—Walker Moore, seat number five."

"Would that I could, but I do not live in the district, Walker," Fisher said, walking into the elevator. "And I don't have any children or any stake in this election."

"Sure you do, the story's your stake, you bitter rat bastard!" the Last Wildcatter roared at Fisher, meekly waiting for the elevator door to close before roaring. The roar was an attempt to get into his lion character, as the theatre professors had coached Walker to do. Walker changed into his freshly dry-cleaned costume and went through his lines again as the cowardly lion. He concentrated on the parody of the *Wizard of Oz* song he would sing alone, *a capella* to a den of critics—including his own critical spouse. First place for funniest sketch at the Synergy International Conference was a trip with spouses for the whole team to New York City for two nights, all expenses paid. Dreaded second place was a trip for the whole team to the World's Biggest Rattlesnake Roundup in Central Texas from whence all returned reeducated, both more conscious of and cowed by their own runner-up weakness, and one team member usually bitten.

After a final inspection in the bathroom mirror and a better than average recitation of his lines, the Last Wildcatter ascended the stage again to accept the first place trophy. His acceptance speech was cut short when Walker made the mistake of looking to his left as he exited the bathroom to see if anyone was in the War Room. Through the conference room glass, the CEO and chief operations officer motioned for the lion to join them.

"What did the reporter want?" the chief operations officer asked. Formerly short, paunchy, bald, married, and with giant eyeglasses, the chief operations officer had recently undergone a reinvention. Now single, slimmed down, a recipient of laser eye surgery, and a participant in extreme sports, he had adopted the cockiness of a jock.

"Nothing," Walker said. "Some information for an article on the school board race."

"*Another* article?" the chief operations officer asked.

Walker's hope that they had not seen the article in the *Chronicle* vanished. Somewhere in the land of pipe dreams the hope floated just behind his interrupted acceptance speech.

"We were just wargaming here, Walker," the CEO said in his fatherly way. His affected tortoise manner fit the Midwestern minister's face he had inherited, but did little to mask the political ambitions that had served him so well in his rise. "Did you know that one month ago today was the anniversary of the fall of the Alamo?"

"I was unaware, sir."

"I thought you were a history buff."

"I am," Walker said, nodding his lion's head. "I've been immersed in the Sundance Oil & Gas deal. Plus my son and his Jefferson High School baseball team are in the playoffs. The Alamo is my favorite battle." Walker was pleased to steer the conversation back to sacred ground. "The greatest moral victory in our country's history. A victory in the sense, too, that it bought the Army of Texas and Sam Houston the time to regroup and defeat Santa Anna and his Mexican army at the Battle of San Jacinto."

"The Alamo was a massacre!" the chief operations officer interjected. Walker knew for a fact the Connecticut-born chief operations officer's mother was not a Daughter of the Alamo. His view of history would be a good deal better informed, thought Walker, if his mother had sung to him—just once—the ballad of "The Thirteen Days of Glory at the Siege of Alamo" before bed, as Walker's mother had done each night for a young Walker. "A spanking at the hands of Mexicans. We translate a moral victory as a fucking loss at Synergy."

"You represent Synergy, Walker," the CEO said pointing to the red Synergy logo on the wall of the War Room.

"Not just the most innovative energy company in the world—the most innovative *company* in the world," the chief operations officer added.

"The Alamo was a defeat," the CEO said. "But the men, all one hundred eighty-nine that chose to stay and fight, did possess courage."

"They wouldn't have let some punk kid humiliate them, and they sure as hell wouldn't have allowed him to humiliate a Texas company like Synergy," the chief operations officer added. "Remember the Alamo."

"We hate bad press here," the CEO said. "How is it coming with Sundance Oil & Gas?"

"I'm a little hesitant about the price, what with the troubling political unrest in Bolivia, where ten percent of their hard assets are. It is impossible to say what the country will look like two years from now."

"It is impossible to say what *this* country will look like in two years! The deal is a steal," the chief operations officer said, slamming the table with his hands. "Close it now and have the accountants use mark-to-market and put it all on this quarter's earnings. Get Donovan Kirby to enter into an exclusive agreement so he doesn't ditch us for a better deal, but leave us a way out. Tell him we want to be the white knight. Stop wavering, Walker, and pull the trigger. This isn't one of your polo matches. Draw a line in the sand. You can't play the cowardly lion all your life."

Walker held out his paws. "I'm in character as the cowardly lion."

"Who is playing you as the brainless scarecrow?" the chief operations officer asked.

"Play the white knight, Walker," the CEO said. "We both know there is no silver medal. The next day people only remember the victor. That's why we highly discourage the notion of second place at Synergy."

"He's right, Walker," the chief operations officer said. "I was reading a fascinating article in a science journal about how rattlesnake venom is disproportionally potent in the blood of the anxiety-ridden types who waiver and finish in second place."

— - — - —

The restored elegance of the Crystal Ballroom terrace of the old Rice Hotel refracted the chaos of the street. A floor underneath the wrought-iron, wrap-around balcony, understaffed valets in black pants, white shirts, and bowties scrambled to open doors for men in tuxedos and women in always-seasonal furs, hustling cars in and out from the parking garage three streets over in an elaborately choreographed dance with one partner forever out of step and winded. In a white tuxedo jacket and bowtie and holding a Dr Pepper on the rocks, Tucker monitored the situation from the terrace approvingly. Many were the foreign sports cars of the manual transmission sort that had befuddled Tucker on his first valet event at the George R. Brown Convention Center the week before. Tucker had lurched the dying cars only inches forward at a time—until acrid smoke signals from multiple car hoods had marked Tucker's self-promotion from valet to supervisor position during the arrival phase where, Tucker assessed, Lagniappe Valet Parking leadership was missing.

Tucker sipped his drink and supervised as the arrival rush below slowed to a trickle. Elliott transitioned from a run to a jog crossing the street, his skin visibly reddish beneath his sweat-soaked white shirt. Edwin and Kingsley Curry waited with tickets in hand to tear off for the next arriving car, the twins making their debut valet outing after Tucker brokered their hiring. Tucker would need the conserved energy in two hours when he would decide as supervisor to switch back to being a regular valet to bring around cars—automatics only—and collect a share of the tips. In all three directions from the terrace, thousands of office lights indicated the presence of other supervisors still at work in downtown Houston.

"Son," a freckled man with hair to match the reddish glow of his lit cigar said, "you're the sharpest-dressed lad here. White bowtie and white dinner jacket. I admire your style."

"The jacket is my father's."

"Look at all that lovely energy being consumed. It is a city of energy, this city, light shining on the believers in the capital of the everyman. Most make their fame or their fortune, and then leave Houston. But why would you want to leave a place with this much energy to tap into? That's what I love about her, Houston, she never runs out. Donovan Kirby."

"No, she doesn't." Tucker took the extended hand like a secret sharer. "Tuck Davis, Director of Attending Valets, candidate for Memorial Independent School District school board seat number five, Mr. Kirby." Tucker turned back towards the ballroom. "This place would make a great place for a rally."

"And for a slaughter," Donovan said. "It is a great location for celebrations, too. You can't call tonight a rally. Tonight's a party. Rallies are for when people need rallying. You can't hold a rally when times are good."

"That's about to change." Tucker set his empty glass down and walked back through the ballroom and down the stairs. Downstairs, the valets lounged around the Rice Hotel entrance in two groups, the veterans and the new Jefferson High School students.

"All right, gather around," Tucker said. "I know y'all ain't made any money tonight so far and times ain't good for us valets." Tucker beckoned the veteran valets to come closer in. The four veterans, men in their late twenties and thirties, waited for the next arriving car.

"There is not a finer week than this week for a rally. Got school until three every day for the next three days, but free after that for rallies," Tucker said. He climbed up on a chair.

"Tucker, no speeches at work," Elliott said.

"It's what this town needs right now," Tucker said. "The energy is there for a rally. I heard it again tonight. We've got to campaign and get the message out there. Rallying is when people rally!"

As Walker grabbed the ticket from the valet with his paw, using his other paw to hold his tail from dragging, he broke from character to recite a line to himself, "You're a closer, a winner, an elected president, and a lion of courage—the courage to play a cowardly lion with no rival in the jungle for first place."

"Every kid a king!"

King of the jungle, hearing the cry again, turned and saw in white his rival for the second straight night. Walker recoiled as if bitten by a rattlesnake.

Three

Tucker pressed up the Randalson's Grocery Store bread aisle with bowlegs wide, decided on the back of the bakery, and ducked behind trays of fresh bread. He picked up the phone attached to the wall in the bakery after sampling the freshness of two pumpkin bread loaves and, not for the first time, pushed the 9 button with sticky pumpkin fingers.

"Sacker Carlos Ortega, please report to the break room immediately," punctuated the classical music playing over the store's ceiling speakers.

"You have to be kidding me!" Carlos Ortega cried when he entered the break room. "What are you doing here, Tucker?"

Tucker inspected the Randalson's Grocery Store Employee of the Month board in his white dinner jacket and bowtie and said, "I never did make it up on the wall of fame."

"How could you have?" Carlos asked. "You were the worst sacker I've ever worked with."

"It sure is good to see you, Carlos." Tucker smiled at the sight of his old friend and former colleague who combed his hair in a 1950s ducktail and wore the whitest Randalson's employee shirt in the store. Carlos Ortega was what Tucker thought of as a nuts-and-bolts kid who believed in ironing his uniform and punching out on the time clock for breaks. It had been a worried Carlos who first warned Tucker he was going to get fired if Tucker continued reading books about Louisiana politics in the break room. "You know, Carlos, when a sacker knows half the customers coming in here, you can't fault him for getting sidetracked as a public relations man. Basic politics, Carlos. All politics is local."

"*Loco* for you," Carlos said. "You're right, Tuck. You weren't the worst sacker. You were the worst employee in the history of Randalson's Grocery Stores."

Tucker jiggled and kicked the locked handle of his old employee locker. "What a history this chain has, running off neighborhood mom and pop grocery stores like the ones we used to know as kids."

"We are kids," Carlos responded to the public relations line from Tucker. "If Mr. Honeycutt sees you back here, he'll probably call the cops and have you arrested. I heard him just last week telling one of the new managers the story about your abrupt resignation before he could fire you."

"'Resignation of Catfish Davis announced, effective when read,'" Tucker proudly quoted from memory the last line of his resignation letter. Tucker examined the selection inside the employees' refrigerator. "You think he would call the cops? That would be a public relations disaster."

"He would still love to fry Catfish."

"I bet the old son of a bitch would love to, if he could only catch me. Tell him I'll be the kid in white fighting for the little folks and the moms and pops. I couldn't help but notice it says on the schedule up there that you are sacking Thursday night."

"What about Thursday night?" Carlos asked. "You better get out of here before Mr. Honeycutt catches you."

"That is why I am going to need you."

— - — - —

The inspiration arrived during lunch on Thursday from Fisher's first journalistic beat, Jefferson High School's, *The Pony Express*, by way of Tucker's courier. Fisher teased the kid courier in the *Chronicle* newsroom about not being in school. The courier informed Fisher he had a hall pass from the class president and told Fisher to check out the third page if he was so curious about things. The courier disappeared as quickly as he had appeared in the newsroom. Fisher opened the school paper at his desk and read the profile of school board candidate Tucker Davis. Pure propaganda, it listed School Board President Moore's failures side by side Tucker's achievements as senior class president, and coupled it with a large picture of the student school board candidate in suit and tie behind the counter shaking hands with the lunch ladies in violation of every state health code. On the opposite page, an editorial endorsed Tucker Davis three weeks before the election.

The inspiration Fisher found was on the back page of the profile, an article on the Memorial TIRZ by a girl with the byline Editor-in-Chief. Fisher barged in and presented the article to his editor. "One more article, but focused on the Memorial TIRZ and the candidates' views. This is the angle missing from my school board race articles."

"*The Pony Express*?" the editor asked. He put the school paper down and continued applying tape to the handle of his tennis racket. "This is what you have been reduced to, getting your leads from a high school paper? I told you already, there is no more blood to squeeze from this school board turnip."

Fisher decided against referencing the passage in the profile in which Tucker claims to bleed genuine Long blood. "There's a story in this TIRZ. And I know there is a story in this kid, chief. I know it."

"Would you settle down, please. This newfound excitement of yours is scaring me, Hughes. The paper retained you all these years because you were our token gay cynic."

"We've run two articles. Why not a third to round it out? I've got a nose for this, and I can smell it."

"Where has this enthusiasm been these last several years? Why don't you just go run his campaign, Fisher? You do have one gargantuan nose, and it is your own exposed ass you smell. The school board race articles have run their course. The last time I let you lead with your nose, you produced a series of articles on a candidate for mayor who had legally renamed himself after an outlaw in a movie."

"Tax zones like this are for severely blighted areas," Fisher said, ignoring the attacks on his sensitive aquiline nose. "How can anyone say one of the richest areas in the country is in need of desperate salvation?"

"This kid candidate says the same thing, talking about all the poor people—that we know don't exist—out there in Memorial not being represented." The editor threw the paper across the desk at Fisher. "Get out of here with your piss and vinegar and go probe this TIRZ. Find me something with that deranged beak of yours besides a smelly catfish."

— - — - —

Carlos sacked the groceries in the wider paper bags. Two registers over, Mr. Honeycutt overrode an error with his store manager key and walked back into his office past the Randalson's customer service booth. Trained incorrectly by Tucker that the number one concern of a sacker was to be always mindful of the location of the manager, the habit stuck with Carlos. But never before had Carlos monitored Mr. Honeycutt as if on a mission, nor had he been corrected by consecutive customers for his misplacement of tomatoes in bags.

Carlos sacked the four empty glass bottles of chocolate milk returned for a bottle deposit in a plastic bag. He handed the bag of bottles to the cashier to place under the register for later collection. Had Carlos been Tucker, he would have brought the milk bottles back an hour later to another cash register to pay for a new bottle of chocolate milk and a candy bar on an unauthorized break. Carlos pushed the cart of sacked groceries behind the perfume trail of the woman who avoided conversation and, thus, the guilt of not tipping.

Carlos returned the empty shopping cart to the west end parking lot cart holder. He took the opportunity of being away from the registers to attend the rally in the far east end of the lot. Carlos had been assigned by Tucker to keep an eye on Mr. Honeycutt and keep him inside, away from the rally. With Mr. Honeycutt safely inside his office, Tucker, sporting a two-button white suit and yellow tie with white polka dots, stood in the back of a white pickup truck and addressed a small crowd. Another kid to the right of Tucker held a handmade campaign poster attached to a thin piece of wood. Inside the parking lot, people listened curiously for a minute before walking into the store with faces, Carlos registered, unsure of what they just witnessed. Carlos spotted one familiar face in the crowd, a tan old man with a great oil-slick silver mane who never dressed in anything but the same white short-sleeved shirt tucked into blue pants. The old man visited the store every day, rambled to every worker he could on any subject, and referred to himself as the Silver Fox.

"If there is anyone who knows, it is Tuck Davis, who once sacked your groceries," Tucker said. He held his palms out. "With these same sacking hands, I will chop down Walker Moore and any other school board representative who rolls around in the same slop. Because it has gotten out of hand. The little folks like y'all ain't represented anymore in your own district. I want to know who is going to get down that jam for y'all from the top shelf—a sacker or some corporate fat cat?"

"He's a kid, but he's right!" Silver Fox yelled to the crowd. He swung a rolled-up magazine. "A working man is what we want in office."

"Tuck Davis is the best friend the working man ever had. But if y'all read yesterday's paper, they say in there, 'Tucker Davis has got no new policies or ideas.' President Moore's own words. Maybe he should come here and meet the folks of his district instead of hiding behind his throne. My policy is that the salt of the earth deserve good education too. Does that make me crazy?"

"No," the kid holding the sign said. Carlos guessed the kid took *crazy* as his cue.

"You think Walker Moore has ever rolled up his sleeves and sacked groceries after a long day of school like Tuck Davis?" Tucker asked the crowd. Carlos abstained from answering and encouraging this line of attack, knowing Tucker had only worked in the summer and his sacking had been minimal.

"No!" the Silver Fox answered.

Carlos walked over behind the Silver Fox who drifted closer and closer to Tucker. Both in white from the waist up, Tucker and the Silver Fox resembled a sales team, though it was not clear to Carlos what they were selling.

"Paper or plastic?" Tucker asked. "Y'all think Walker Moore ever asked that question? Maybe he thinks—"

"It is what is wrong with America!" the Silver Fox cried as though he had been thrust into the pulpit to deliver a sermon. "They do not let this boy stand, rather they attack him for fighting—"

"Thank you, brother, for your endorsement," Tucker said to the Silver Fox. Neither Tucker nor Carlos noticed Mr. Honeycutt zeroing in on them across the parking lot with the Town and Country Shopping Center security guard. Forty feet away on Memorial Drive, people bogged down in perpetual Houston standstill traffic lowered their windows facing the open parking lot. "Like I was telling my good friend Elliott here holding the sign, this man has got a point about—"

"The point is the politicians only care about themselves," the Silver Fox wailed, overcome with a new anger. "Just look at this slick draft-dodging President we got. He doesn't care a lick about us suffering down here, too busy with his own affairs." The Silver Fox continued his joust on another field with an unseen opponent. "We need to sweep out this government and get one that leaves us alone. A government that doesn't tax one hundred and ten cents on the dollar and more!"

"Let the candidate speak!" Carlos shouted. "Davis for School Board!" Carlos felt a tap on his shoulder and turned around.

"What are you doing, Carlos?" Mr. Honeycutt asked. "What the hell is going on out here?"

"What's going on is we're trying to get a little representation without the taxation from you!" the Silver Fox answered, hell bent on throwing all the tea into the harbor of the parking lot.

"Remove this man and arrest that kid," Mr. Honeycutt said to the security guard, pointing at the Silver Fox and the sacker masked in a white suit who Mr. Honeycutt had been robbed the chance of firing. "No demonstrations are allowed on Randalson's private property. All who instigate demonstrations will be banned from Randalson's and have charges filed against them."

"Do not tread on us," the Silver Fox said to the thinning crowd.

Elliott tugged at the cuffed pant leg of Tucker and said, "I think it is about time to move on to the next rally and get the hell out of here."

"I'm right behind you," Tucker said.

While the security guard tried to get the Silver Fox to put down the rolled-up magazine he was swinging, Tucker stepped down from the pickup and slipped away with Elliott. Tucker motioned to Carlos to meet him in the back at the loading docks.

"We have a right to free speech. This kid is a candidate for public office," the Silver Fox said, pointing to the empty truck bed Tucker had vacated.

"You do not have this right here," Mr. Honeycutt said. "You are no longer allowed on Randalson's property."

"I have been a customer here at Randalson's since its opening thirty years ago," the Silver Fox said. "Is this how you treat your senior citizens?"

"There are no exceptions to the policy, I'm afraid, even for senior citizens," Mr. Honeycutt said. "What were you doing out here participating, Carlos?"

"Are you really banning the Silver Fox, Mr. Honeycutt?" Carlos asked. The security guard ushered away the magazineless Silver Fox. "He's been here every day that I've worked the past two years."

"Yes," Mr. Honeycutt said, "and you can join him, because you're fired."

"I already resigned during the rally," Carlos lied, happy to sabotage any satisfaction Mr. Honeycutt derived from firing him. Carlos took off his Randalson's nametag and flicked it at the ground at his feet. The plastic badge bounced twice on the pavement, disappointingly not sticking in the dirt like a sheriff's tin star in a Western. Nor did grateful townspeople run out to greet him after the gunfight.

Tucker and Elliott waited for Carlos by the loading docks dumpster. Flies swarmed over a crate of rotten produce next to the overflowing dumpster. Tucker introduced Carlos to Elliott, who Carlos recognized as the sign-holder at the rally.

"Sounded like they banned that old coot and carted

him off to the mental hospital. Real firecracker and loose cannon," Tucker said, shaking his head. "He kept cutting me off and stealing the floor from me at the rally. I was telling Elliott that I think that old man might be crazy." He jerked his thumb behind him in the direction of Randalson's and asked, "Was it really necessary for them to show up armed and tell us we can't rally in the parking lot?"

"I just got fired," Carlos said.

"Good," Tucker said, "because I've got a job for you."

— - — - —

The Petroleum Club on the forty-fourth floor of the downtown Exxon building was, Walker Moore told friends he invited to dine, the best place in town for a drink. From a chair at the Wildcatter Grill, a selection of the best scotch in the world could be enjoyed with a view of Houston out to the ship channel refineries through floor-to-ceiling glass windows. The Houston humidity, Walker would claim after a few drinks, served to trap the smog between the twentieth and fortieth floors. The Last Wildcatter was on his third drink in a half hour at the Wildcatter Grill and feeling as trapped as the smog when Skip Brammer plopped down at his table. Even with the gray in his full head of salt-and-pepper hair, the real estate lawyer and city councilman flashed the same youthful expression that conned Walker into helping him lure a borrowed cow up to the third floor of their high school library.

Skip gestured to the waiter to bring them two more drinks and said to Walker, "Guess which old classmate I just talked with."

After several guesses and lengthy deliberations between guesses, Skip tired and told Walker. "He talked with you too today?" Walker asked. "About the TIRZ?"

"What else would that queer be talking to me for?"

"He's gay?"

"I'm sure the faggot is fighting against the Memorial TIRZ." Skip slapped Walker on the knee and smiled. "Do you remember when the district was forced to use a crane to remove both a section of the library roof and the cow that refused to go down the stairs?"

Like the cow in the senior prank fable he enabled, Walker dug in and refused to descend at the slapping. "I am worried about the way we are intent on approaching the TIRZ and passing it as quickly as possible without any debate."

"You're not starting to feel the heat from a crazy high school student, are you? Stop worrying about some loser kid and start thinking about your future in Washington. You can't show any doubt or weakness in a congressional race, or it will be like a feeding frenzy of sharks tearing apart a cow. There is no lifeline, or crane, if you are the cow. The big leagues, Walker."

"When I was up at Jefferson this week, Skip, I spoke to a government class and a small girl asked me how I can honestly consider Memorial a poor area. I told her to ask you, since you are the expert on real estate law. So I'm asking you, how is Memorial poor?"

"Don't you see it *will* be poor if the TIRZ doesn't pass? Memorial will be left behind and business will go outside the city to the suburbs like Katy, The Woodlands, Sugarland, and the newer commercial property out there on cheaper land."

"Houston is a real-estate developer's wet dream. We're the only major city in America without zoning laws. We're overdeveloped and overdeveloping. Maybe we need some restrictions and law and order for a change before we consume the whole city with TIRZs."

"The Houston Dream that made this city so livable and gave us our unique identity is under threat if we don't pass the TIRZ."

"The solution is to give tax breaks and write corporate welfare checks to Memorial National?"

"Jesus H. Christ, Fisher Hughes did a number on you today. Dreamers like Fisher are against TIRZs so the neighborhoods can stay artsy, so the character and culture is preserved in falling down old houses and buildings. A romantic notion we, as the leaders of this city, do not have the luxury to indulge. I saw a wooden boat last week lost in a weed-filled lot off Waugh that looked like it could have been sailed up the bayou on the Allen Brothers' expedition. That is not progress."

Walker walked over to lean against the glass window, the vastness of Houston laid out.

Skip joined Walker at the window. "We have the chance to give birth to development, to revitalize the city we love. The Brammer and Moore families have always presided as powerbrokers of development and done what is best for Houston. It was why we were elected. We send people to the moon in this city." Skip pointed out beyond the downtown skyline with his drink. "Look at the majestic colors of this sunset."

"I think that is the petrochemicals in the smog," Walker said.

"You do not see smog from the forty-fourth floor of the Petroleum Club."

A driller, all for development, Walker searched his summer as an oil field roughneck for guidance. "I don't know."

"Not everyone gets the opportunity in life to lead such historical change," Skip said. "You are a senior executive at Synergy, the leading company in the city. You know what it means to be a trailblazer. There is no history here besides the history being made. Politics and positive business development together equal a better Houston. It all comes together to equal a better whole. This is the essence of synergy."

Synergy, the Last Wildcatter blushed, was when his fellow roughnecks stopped calling him a "narc" on his last night, got him drunk, and he woke up naked in a whorehouse bed, his boots still on. "I do believe in synergy," Walker said.

— - — - —

"Catfish," the chubby student eating the chili hotdog at the Houston Zoo food stand said, "would probably be in the aquarium." Fisher could not tell if sarcasm lay concealed behind the acne and smeared chili.

After a walk through the aquarium, Fisher found the suited fish next door in the dark reptile house. Tucker scrutinized a two-headed rat snake donated to the zoo after being found in a Houston attic. On the other side of Tucker, Elliott took dictation next to a large albino alligator on exhibit from Louisiana behind thick glass. Fisher thought it was a toss-up between Elliott and the alligator as to who was bigger.

"We need to pass out fliers ahead of the next rally," Tucker said to Elliott writing in a pocketsize notebook.

"Mr. Davis," Fisher said, "I expected to find you outside shaking hands and talking to voters. It does not get any better than a sunny Friday afternoon at the Houston Zoo."

"I was, earlier. We are taking a short lunch break here to plan." Tucker tapped on the glass. "This guy is the only known two-headed rat snake in the world."

"I disagree, I've known a lot of two-headed rat snakes," Fisher said, thinking he had even dated a two-headed rat snake or two in his life. The snake lay next to its flaky papyrus-yellow film of shed skin.

A smile pushed out Tucker's eyes. "Mr. Hughes," Tucker said, shaking hands, "you missed the first rally last night in Memorial."

"How did it go?"

"Well," Elliott said, "we almost got arrested."

"Held it at Randalson's Grocery Store on Memorial Drive,"Tucker said. "Great with the working-class folks."

"Not a lot of those in Memorial though."

"Maybe not yesterday," Tucker said. "But I hired a working-class sacker, Carlos Ortega from Spring Valley High School, as tough as nails, to be a manager of the campaign here with Elliott. We've got him on the team and he's a silky, street-smart orphan."

"He's an orphan?"

"No sisters or brothers like me, just a kid of the people."

Fisher momentarily considered explaining the definition of orphan. But he did not wish to throw water on the burning comet that was Tucker in his inexplicable dragless suits a size too big. He watched Tucker and his awkward gait approach the alligator like they were about to wrestle. It occurred to Fisher that here was an eighteen-year-old both far more confused and determined than he had once been. He was impressed and depressed. "How did you hire another manager?" Fisher asked. "From campaign funds?"

"You could say that. Off the record, I'm back-dooring him a job as a valet after he got fired at Randalson's in exchange for him agreeing to help us campaign north of I-10 on the Spring Branch side. There are votes to be had out there in them hills. Over seventy percent of the students of Memorial Independent School District live in Spring Branch."

"Yet six of seven school board members live in Memorial," Fisher said. He walked over and knocked on the glass between them and the albino alligator. The alligator did not blink an eyelid, unfazed by the three creatures entranced by its whiteness. "Memorial is where the money is and the adults who turn out to vote in the election live. Walker Moore knows that is his base to cover. He's got a strategy."

"We've got a strategy, too," Elliott said, holding up the notebook.

"But without an issue," Fisher said. Fisher slapped the

glass and the alligator raised its head. "What you need to beat Walker Moore is an issue."

"What do you mean?" Tucker asked, his bug eyes narrowing like a fellow resident of the reptile house.

"You have to energize the voters, bring out the voters who never vote. You have to get them passionate about an issue that affects them and makes them want to vote. If I were you, and not a journalist, I would find a hot-button issue, which is not easy in a school board election."

"What hot-button issue would you choose if you were running?" Elliott asked Fisher.

"It's been a long time since I've had to think like a candidate," Fisher said.

"I can whip Walker Moore with one whisker," Tucker said at the alligator. "I'm half alligator, half snapping turtle, all catfish. I could stare the bark off the pine tree that is Walker Moore. I'll let the little folks finish chopping him down after that. I'm a populist, not some puppet. The Last Populist. Last, leastways, holding Texas public office that would bleed Louisiana Long if they shot me on the capitol steps. I will energize the people of the district by letting them know they will finally be represented if they vote for me. I can take Walker Moore, or I'll eat my hat!"

"But what is your take on the Memorial TIRZ and its backer Memorial National?" Fisher asked. Fisher handed Tucker the TIRZ article from *The Pony Express*.

"This is Duna's article. I'm taking her to the prom," Tucker boasted.

"I am doing an article on this controversial issue of the Memorial TIRZ for the Sunday paper and I've already interviewed your opponent and a few other powerful public figures. I have not yet heard from you on the issue. I can tell you they are all in favor of it."

"If Walker Moore is for it, then I am against it," Tucker said.

"Why?"

— - — - —

"What's your answer, Governor Boudreaux, to those critics who will proclaim if you are acquitted, 'Bobby Boudreaux is guilty as sin, but the prosecutors and feds just aren't wily enough to catch him?'" a reporter asked outside the New Orleans Federal Courthouse.

Bobby Boudreaux paused to grin before stepping in the limousine and said to the gathering of reporters, "They're half right."

Inside the limousine, Bobby cursed the events of the courtroom with his lawyer, his chief of staff, his younger brother (also under indictment), and his twenty-eight-year-old wife, Candy. His son, on trial as well in the courthouse for the same charges, rode in a separate limousine. For the first time in his life, Bobby Boudreaux was having a hard time enjoying New Orleans. He faced two hundred thirty years in prison if found guilty on all accounts of racketeering and extortion. At the age of seventy-two, the populist Cajun King from Crowley, Louisiana, was being silenced in his own state.

"This gag order is strangling me and killing my chances to win the jury vote," Bobby complained. "This judge has taken away my strongest defense—making the people laugh at this human comedy at daily press conferences."

"The best was during our first trial when you pulled up driving that horse carriage we borrowed from the French Quarter tour guide," the chief of staff reminisced.

"They are scared, Bobby," his brother said. "They know they can't catch you. This is their latest underhanded tactic. Judge Rizzola is completely on their side."

"I have prepared a strong line of questioning to attack their key witness next week," the lawyer said.

No matter how many times Bobby educated his New York lawyer that legalities were not the true battle in a Louisiana courtroom, the lawyer fell back on the articles of the law. Bobby cursed himself for hiring the hotshot attorney recommended by his confidantes against his better instincts. Caught in midstream, he was stuck with the lawyer. Bobby looked out at the downtown New Orleans skyline, which had not changed at all since he was elected thirty years before during his first run for governor. In his hand, he balled up and squeezed his lucky white and gold handkerchief he wore in his jacket breast pocket.

"Get those damn wiretaps thrown out of court," his brother said to the lawyer. "It is discrediting to Bobby's integrity to listen to him discussing illegal payment delivery."

"I have something y'all might find interesting," Candy declared excitedly. No one in the limousine said anything, out of respect for Bobby. A leggy blonde who had introduced pink mini-skirts into the First Lady of Louisiana wardrobe, Candy rarely raised her soft voice among Bobby's inner circle.

"What is it, my little delta queen?" Bobby asked his wife with hair as immaculate as Bobby's coiffed gray.

Candy read aloud both the letter and article sent from Houston. Again, all in the limousine waited respectfully for Bobby to encourage her to stop talking. Missing the twinkle emerging in his client's eyes, the lawyer resumed their strategizing, "In the end it will hinge on—"

"School board," Bobby murmured, barely audible.

The limousine turned on Annunciation Street and pulled up outside an old white wooden house with a glass door in the back and a yellow sign for po-boy sandwiches. The line of people outside Domilise's drank Dixie beers and laughed, wiggling inside to breathe the frying smell of the best shrimp po-boy sandwich in town. The sun sank a little lower over the Mississippi River to touch the smokestacks of passing ships behind them. The people in line paid no interest to the limousine.

"School board!" Bobby cried to the audience inside the limousine. "It is perfect. Nothing has a more honorable sound in politics. School . . . *board*."

"You are his hero," his brother said, rubbing his hands together. "He supports you one hundred percent and believes in your innocence."

"Just the sort of break and twist we need," the chief of staff said. "It's brilliant."

"He's an underdog, honey," Candy said. "People love underdogs like y'all."

"It is a virtuous quest," the lawyer said, getting in on the game of Louisiana politics.

"I want you on this," Bobby said to his chief of staff. "I need to know everything about this kid and this race. The old country lawyer in me is telling me this is our ticket around the gag order. We will speak straight to the hearts of the people—and hopefully a few jurors—like our young friend in Houston. Candy, save the envelope, we are going to send our underdog a donation. He is like a young me."

"Except you were never innocent," his brother said.

"If he studied at the same School of Long I did," Bobby said, "he's not either."

— - — - —

Elliott and Tucker picked up Duna and Carlos on the north side of I-10 where the Southern Pacific railroad tracks split. Tucker chose Allen's Glen, west of Gessner on Memorial Drive, as the site of the meeting. Named after the Allen Brothers who sailed up the Buffalo Bayou in 1836 to found Houston—the area of Houston then a malarial swamp the two hucksters marketed as a paradise in print advertisements—Allen's Glen was built a century and a half later farther upstream from where historical evidence showed the Allen Brothers to have landed. A small community of brown wooden townhomes, Allen's Glen was an artifice expertly designed to sink into the bayou vegetation. Tucker selected the site because he wanted to show his team where he had spent the first five years of his life kicking about political ideas. Tucker and his campaign staff stood on a hill of sand and observed a three-foot long alligator gar in the bayou, floating in place and using a fallen cypress tree branch to conceal itself from the smaller fish it stalked.

"In 1928, my hero Huey Long became governor," Tucker said. "But as great as ole' Huey was, he got a little help in his rise to power from a controversy surrounding the Great Mississippi River Flood of 1927. You see, the rich folks of New Orleans determined their property was too valuable to flood and that it would be better to sacrifice the little folks below New Orleans. So as the river kept rising and it kept raining, they strong-armed then-Governor of Louisiana O.H. Simpson into dynamiting the levee below New Orleans rather than risk their hides with the little folks. Politics is what washed away the little folks. The little folks never forgot, and the Kingfish never forgot either, dynamiting the moneychangers with the charge of betrayal at every stump speech after that on his way to the governor's seat. I read Duna's beautiful article on the Memorial TIRZ earlier today, and Fisher Hughes is doing another one on it for the Sunday paper. A few want to dynamite the levee again to pass the Memorial TIRZ, but Catfish ain't going to let them."

"What is your plan?" Duna asked. "The city approved it and President Moore said everyone else is in favor of it."

"The school board," Tucker said, "votes on the twenty-third of April on the Memorial TIRZ, but the school board election is the following Monday on the twenty-sixth."

"You need to be careful, Tucker," Duna said. "Memorial National owns more than sixty percent of the land covered in the Memorial TIRZ boundaries. If you attack Walker Moore about the TIRZ, you are attacking Memorial National."

Tucker handed Duna the business card Fisher Hughes gave him. "I want you to write the press release on this one with me, then get it to Mr. Hughes. We're going to dynamite and hit them hard."

"I don't know if I can do this, Tucker—the ethics involved," Duna said. "I'm editor of the paper."

Tucker took off his fedora and touched the hand and milk-white skin—skin paler than his own—of his prom date. "You think I care a lick about your skin color? I know you are Persian, and there are not many Persians at Jefferson High School, but I'll bet my bottom dollar you will be prom queen. There's not a girl more beautiful than you in our senior class or a girl who can write an article so beautiful defending little folks. I've waited two years to say that to you, Duna."

"You waited two years to say anything to her," Elliott added.

"The great thing about this city, y'all," Tucker said, "is that no one cares what side of the tracks you come from."

"*Ethics*," Duna said, touching Tucker with her other hand not in his grasp. "Not *ethnics*, Tucker. It could be perceived as unethical and morally wrong to write for both."

The alligator gar thrashed violently in the brown water. The murky water settled, a skewered sunfish in the snout of teeth.

"Neither ethnics," Tucker said, thinking of the poor people of every stripe and color Huey fought for, "nor ethics were anything the Kingfish ever worried much about when he went about taking down the moneychangers. If it takes dynamite to kick out the moneychangers who would dynamite the little folks, then by God, Catfish will use dynamite. But like the gar, we are going to dynamite in phases before we go in for the kill. The only thing unethical is being in the right in a fight and getting cowed by the wrong. This ain't government class, this is politics. The virtue of Huey Long teaches us that you got to be willing to use dynamite against them who would use dynamite against the little folks."

They watched the gar disappear into the muddy water. Tucker returned the fedora to the crown of his head and slid down to the base of the sandy hill on the bank of the bayou. He dug the heel of his right brown dress shoe in the sand to write SCHOOL BOARD. Tucker looked across at the campaigners who had followed him thus far and said, "I understand populist politics ain't for everyone, and there ain't no shame in that. If y'all want to leave the class legacy with me, it is going to get rough, I reckon. We're standing in a district surrounded by Memorial National and the moneychangers who have already bet the bank on running it.

"But I know we've got a team here among us, a political team in talent and friends even tougher than the Share Our Wealth Coalition I organized that took down water. Hell, maybe the critics are right in that I'm getting too old to be loose and going it alone in these fights. But I'm in whole hog, and I'd like to get in this fight as a team and leave a legacy the little folks of this district won't ever forget. Not everyone gets the chance in life to make a stand and leave a legacy."

"What do we want to title the press release?" Duna asked, crossing the divide of silence created by Tucker's lines in the sand.

"Present the voters with a choice," Elliott said. "Give them a question, something like . . ."

Carlos suggested, "Every kid a king or every crook a contract?"

"*Crony* instead of crook," Tucker corrected Carlos. Tucker ascended back up the hill to join the campaign team.

He put his arm around his friend's shoulder and with the pride of a father said to Carlos, "That reminds me, I got you a valet job tomorrow night at the Alley Theatre. You will be working alongside Edwin and Kingsley Curry, two of the strongest loyalists in my network."

Four

"We passed the tax incremental reinvestment zone because it is what is best for the city. You have elected me three times as mayor to do what is best for the city," Mayor Lanny Whiting said.

"I live in Memorial, in a home three blocks from the home I grew up in," Skip Brammer added from the side of the podium in the city hall lobby. "The Memorial TIRZ will bring development to the area, which will snowball into more development, which will raise the value of the homes and make for a better neighborhood and better city, one neighborhood at a time."

"What is your response, Mayor Whiting, to the article in yesterday's paper that your position in favor of the Memorial TIRZ is against the will of the people?" a reporter asked.

"I have not had a chance to read the paper yet as I have been focused, as you all know, on getting a new resolution passed to add more police officers to the force to combat crime and lower the homicide rate, so I will not be able to comment on it at this time."

"Councilman Brammer, what do you say to the fact that Memorial National, which owns sixty percent of the land affected by the Memorial TIRZ, stands to save three hundred thirty-four million dollars at the expense of the taxpayers with the specialized tax incentives?"

"The whole idea behind it is to give tax incentives to kick-start development, billions of dollars of development. Memorial National happens to be a large commercial land owner and one of the developers that could generate a lot of business for the area and the city in the Memorial TIRZ under consideration. Next question."

"According to Tucker Davis, a recently-declared candidate for Memorial Independent School District school board, 'The problem of the Memorial TIRZ starts with the fat cats at city hall and their closeness to commercial real estate companies like Memorial National. Trusting Councilman Brammer or Mayor Whiting on the issue of tax incremental reinvestment zones would be like asking a flock of buzzards to watch a ham you just bought for your family at the store and paid tax on—they would not only eat it all in their untouchable special roost protected by new laws, but lie to you afterwards about a wolf stealing it with the stench of carrion all over their feathers and without offering you a dime for it, then reinvest the money they saved from your troubles in more roosts for the future. The Memorial TIRZ stinks and so do the politicians at city hall and that is the way Memorial National likes it. They would rather buy the buzzards than be honest with the people of this city and pay their tax dime.'"

"That is the most ridiculous thing I have heard all year," Skip Brammer said. "The candidate you reference is an eighteen-year-old kid who—"

"Buzzards," Mayor Whiting said, brushing Skip Brammer aside to get back to the microphone. "I hope you are watching this press conference at home on your television, Mr. Davis. It is obvious you have no clue as to what you are talking about and simply enjoy causing trouble. When you lose your current race, come run for mayor this fall against this buzzard and I will beat you so badly you will regret ever having waded into the contact sport that is city politics."

"Give it to him, Lanny!" Mrs. Moore cheered Mayor Whiting on the television screen in the summer kitchen, reminding Walker again that his attacks fared poorly in comparison to the mayor's assault. Walker looked away from his wife and back to the pile of smelly mulch that awaited him on his day off. His wife had a way of finding mulch with the least bark and the most animal chips. "Why don't you grow a pair of balls and attack him like Mayor Whiting? Stop being a punching bag and act like an oilman. God bless, it is embarrassing to be your wife, Walker. That is enough television for you. Roll up your sleeves. I've got a job for you."

A day off was never a day off, Walker accepted early in his marriage. Today his wife insisted on spreading mulch around the azaleas. Walker doubted his wife would even know what an azalea was had he not rescued her from the battered, double-wide trailer in West Texas oil-patch country to live among the azaleas of Memorial.

— - — - —

"I really do not know about this, Tuck," Elliott said. Elliott, Tucker, and Carlos sat in the cab of Elliott's pickup truck in the parking lot of the Shady Oaks retirement home.

"You're my right-hand man, my vice president," Tucker said.

"This does not fall under the job responsibilities of vice president."

"It falls under the responsibilities of best friend."

"I refuse to allow you to invoke our friendship to support your craziness," Elliott said. "Do you know how many times you would have gotten your ass kicked if it weren't for me?"

"How long have we been best friends?"

"Since the first week of first grade when you got us sent to the principal's office for trading baseball cards during class."

"That's right," Tucker said. "I completely ripped you off in that trade, too, if you remember. But who fell on his sword in the principal's office and took all the blame?"

"That's because it was entirely your fault."

"I'm as loyal as a bulldog."

"How would you know? You've never even had a dog."

"All those years and the things we've been through, and it doesn't even compare to the fight we're facing now. I couldn't have picked a more loyal team to get into a fight with. And what do you care, you're going to Yale."

"I didn't even apply to Yale," Elliott said. "Look, my mom sent me here to drop off the pictures we forgot to drop off last week, that's it."

"Your mom is not running for office like we are," Tucker said. "Ask yourself, 'What do you think the Governor would do?'"

"What governor?" Elliott asked. "What are you talking about?"

"I'm talking about politicking."

"No one else is talking about politicking, Tuck. These people are old," Elliott said, gesturing in the direction of two old men who sat outside on a bench at the entrance of the retirement home.

Tucker rolled down his window and tipped his fedora. The two men tipped their hats. "When are you kids going to learn that old folks got a say in this government?" Tucker asked Elliott and Carlos. "I never even got to meet my grandmother or grandfather like y'all, or stir them up over politics. Old folks are the truest little folks we got in this district. We wouldn't even be here fighting this fight if it weren't for old folks like the people of Shady Oaks. I thought we were a team, y'all."

"You're not obligated to do this," Elliott said to Carlos, who opened the truck door to follow Tucker. "He's been playing the loyalty card for twelve years now."

"They are voters and he needs votes, Elliott," Carlos said.

Elliott got out of the truck and looked up to the sky. "I am the crazy one."

A search found Granny Taylor in the Shady Oaks cafeteria at lunch with friends. Tucker estimated three hundred voters dined at the tables. Inside next to the entrance doors, a tiny lady in a yellow and white flower dress for a day in church held a microphone and read a poem in front of two large black speakers several inches taller than her. The people at the tables closest paid some attention to the poetry while everyone in the cafeteria ate. On the other side of Granny Taylor, Tucker stuffed chicken fried steak in his mouth and explained his rules for a good gravy.

"It ain't the fact that no one can cook a good gravy like y'all anymore that worries me," Tucker said. He grabbed his fedora from his knee and stood up at the table. "It's the gravy train rolling through this district of ours right now. A gravy train big and streamlined and fast as hell."

"This is a cafeteria. A lady just finished reading a poem," Elliott said. "This is not the place for school board politics."

"For more reasons than one," Carlos said, pointing to the back of a brochure he had picked up in the lobby. "Memorial National owns this place. What does it not own?"

Tucker read the back of the brochure. The Memorial National monopoly stared Tucker in the face the way the Standard Oil Company had Huey Long. He threw down the brochure on the table. "Doesn't own us or the little folks of Shady Oaks."

"They told us two weeks ago that we might have to move in the fall in order to expand the mall and shopping centers," Granny Taylor said.

"Does Dad know?" Elliott asked.

Granny Taylor shook her head and said, "Nothing is definitive yet, Elliott."

"It will be when Memorial National gets the tax break of a lifetime for commercial development," Elliott said.

"Granny Taylor, do they still offer the bus service to events?" Tucker asked.

"Yes," Granny Taylor said, "but you need at least twenty-five signatures of people who want to go."

"Mrs. Taylor, how many people live here at Shady Oaks?" Carlos asked.

"About three hundred fifty people, son. This is most of us in here."

"Maybe this is a place for politics," Elliott said to Tucker.

"It will be a place for politics when Memorial National takes a wrecking ball to the place, but at that point that doesn't do the residents sitting here any good," Carlos said.

"They're going to have to take a wrecking ball to me first before I let them lay a finger on Granny Taylor, the only grandparent beside the Kingfish I've ever known," Tucker said. He aligned his tie and buttoned the lowest right button of his bronze double-breasted suit. Tucker walked over and picked up the wireless microphone and waited for the crowd to simmer down.

"I think he is wearing your wedding suit," a wag at the front table howled to a man sitting next to him who replied, "He better not be—that's the suit you're supposed to bury me in."

"I reckon most of y'all don't know me. I'm Tuck Davis, but y'all can call me Catfish. I'm running for school board."

"*Catfish*," the wag repeated, earning laughter at his table.

"And I just might be the only friend you folks have got in politics."

Tucker cut up the middle where the tables were parted. He tossed his hat to Carlos and circled through the cafeteria.

He softened them up with a story Huey Long used to tell crowds about hooking up an old family horse to the buggy carriage and taking his Catholic grandparents to mass at seven o'clock, and then bringing them home, and hitching up the horse again at ten and taking his Baptist grandparents to church. Getting into character as Huey Long, Tucker delivered the punch line to a political boss in response to dismay at learning Long was half Catholic, "*Don't be a damned fool, we didn't even have a horse.*"

Half Catholic, half Jewish Tucker Davis stopped in the middle. "Raise a hand if y'all know who Walker Moore is." No hands moved. "I want y'all to meet him tonight. He is someone y'all should have a good look at, though I will give my lucky fifty-cent piece to the first person he looks back in the eye." Tucker held up the playground-collected silver coin he pulled from his jacket breast pocket. "I want y'all to get a good look tonight at Walker Moore because he is my opponent in the school board election and no friend of Shady Oaks. We're going to have a little get-together at seven at the district administration building, and it would mean a lot to me if y'all were there. All of the members of the school board headed by President Moore will be there. Do not go on account of Tuck Davis. Go on account of the fact that if the school board votes to approve the Memorial TIRZ plan, there ain't going to be any Shady Oaks in the new tax incremental reinvestment zone. Y'all think Walker Moore has a plan for the little folks? Why, he can't even bring himself down here to give y'all the time of day and answer any questions y'all might have."

The woman in the yellow and white flower dress raised her hand.

"Yes, ma'am," Tucker said. "Fire away."

"Are you a Republican or a Democrat?" the woman asked.

"Am I a freshwater or saltwater catfish? I ain't anything

but Catfish and a friend of yours with a fin for stinging our enemies."

"That's good enough for me."

"I can see most of the ladies look a lot younger than me and won't be old enough to vote. But I would greatly appreciate it if those of y'all who are older than me and eligible to vote would please register so you can vote in the election on the twenty-sixth of this month."

A man in the back leaned on a walker and asked, "How are you going to stop Memorial National? It owns Shady Oaks, and if it wants to build here, it will build here. There is no stopping that. Raising trouble will only make it harder on us while we are still here."

"Memorial National's got the itch to build because it is about to get the sweetest sweetheart deal this city has ever cut a corporation. Suddenly Shady Oaks is not profitable enough? Hell, I'd build too if I could cut the taxes to nothing in the richest area of town and save half a billion dollars. But y'all tell the school board tonight they will all be thrown out of office if they approve it, and I can guarantee y'all it won't pass because all the buzzards want to save their own necks. All the money Memorial National has given them will be forgotten when they realize they are about to no longer be in office. And y'all will be the folks to clean them out."

"Or they will clean you and pick the bones," the wag said. "I saw Mayor Whiting on television this morning and he called you a troublemaker!"

Tucker pressed his hands down in the air to tamp the rising noise in the cafeteria. "The mayor and city hall don't scare me."

"He is a troublemaker," a voice shouted above the noise of the crowd from the back of the cafeteria.

In a white shirt and blue pants, the voice and hair unmistakable, the crazy man from Randalson's barreled with his chest out in front of his legs toward Tucker. How could the old man be released already from the mental institute? Believing the old man was a plant by Memorial National to derail his campaign, Tucker unbuttoned the lowest right button on his double-breasted jacket for battle.

The Silver Fox approached and yelled, "But he's *our* troublemaker!" Perplexed, Tucker handed over the microphone when the Silver Fox requested it.

"It was this kid that got the Silver Fox banned from Randalson's and damn near arrested," the Silver Fox said. "He is damn good at causing trouble, that's for sure. But he's the only one raising hell for us and causing the trouble—the good trouble—we got to have if we want to one day recognize this area and city of ours. If we want to still have Shady Oaks. Memorial National controls the mall, the shopping strips, city hall, and Shady Oaks, but not the voters who live in Shady Oaks. Who make Shady Oaks what Shady Oaks is. I know he is a kid, but he is the only horse we got running in this race we can bet on. Ain't that right, Catfish?"

"If I said it any sweeter I might be the devil himself," Tucker said. "But I ain't the devil, not yours at least. I reckon I might be the devil to Memorial National and city hall, but then that sort of makes me an angel to y'all. Just like kids are too young, they're going to say you're too old to care about a school board race. What they don't understand is that little folks don't care about color or age, they care about being heard!"

The Silver Fox initiated a slow clap. The clap caught and filled the cafeteria and the people of Shady Oaks joined the Silver Fox and Tucker on their feet. Carlos passed around a sheet for signatures. Elliott left campaign information with Granny Taylor. And Tucker hooked up the horse to the buggy carriage to arrange to take all to the school board meeting in the three Shady Oaks' mini-buses.

— - — - —

The raucous, happy-hour crowd holed up at the Last Concert Cafe demanded more from the hero under the shadow of the traffic-clogged highway. On the corner of William and Nance Streets, the cafe lay in the shade like a homeless person under the off-ramp of the interstate on the outskirts of downtown. A hold-out against downtown expansion, it flew its survivor flag on the sleeves of its loyal patrons who had to knock before being admitted by the matron.

"'Memorial National Incorporated supports the differences of opinion among public servants—'"

"Servants, all right."

Fisher continued to read from the Memorial National press release over the yells of his rowdy colleagues, "'of every political party and hopes the final solution agreed upon represents the best interests of the majority of Houstonians.'"

"And Memorial National."

"'Memorial National supports the continued passage of the Memorial TIRZ as the best opportunity to promote long-term growth in Houston,'" Fisher read aloud. "'Memorial National respects all differing viewpoints and welcomes any dialogue with the community to achieve this shared goal. Memorial National refrains from commenting on the extreme views—'"

"Extreme!"

Fisher read louder, "'of one reporter and one candidate it feels would be better served by addressing the issue at the next meeting of city council or school board.'"

"School board!"

Fisher held up the Memorial National press release like he was holding up his own bounty to mock. "That, kids, is how you write a formal press release." The other reporters from the *Chronicle* called on the renegade reporter for more reading and shooting at the faintly visible moon, a hanging paper chad in the white sky. "Deny all influence, proclaim a shared ambition with the community despite every sign indicating otherwise, and always label the media—and especially your accuser—extreme and, indirectly, crazy. Which might be the one statement of fact in this press release."

"Long live Catfish!"

"We may never see his like again in this town," Fisher eulogized over the top of his fourth drink. From the depths of what unknown bayou this whiskerless catfish had emerged, Fisher did not care. He simply wished to capture the sound and fury of this finned gunslinger. "May he stay with politics."

"More margaritas?" the waitress asked Fisher and the other reporters. She shuttled between them and another table of musicians who hung out under the banana trees and drank cheap Mexican beer with limes and strummed acoustic guitars.

"Yes!" the reporters answered.

"Cut my tab off," Fisher said, "for I have to cover a meeting with the city's finest leaders and one fish who swims against the current."

"Catfish swims again!"

— - — - —

"May I borrow the car, mom?" Tucker asked walking into the kitchen. "I might need to bus some people."

"I don't see why not. We have the Rice Distinguished Alumni Awards Night tonight. One of the awardees is the author Larry McMurtry, so it should be very exciting. I left a package on your bed that was at the house when I came home from the library."

In his room, Tucker opened the package and found another, smaller envelope with a note:

Dear Tucker: The Chinese have a saying, "If you sit by the river long enough, the dead body of your enemy will come floating by." They will have to wait a bit longer for my dead body. Hope the white envelope helps defeat that stuffed-suit opponent of yours. Looking forward to following your march to victory. Yours, Bobby Boudreaux.

Tucker opened the white envelope. Wrapped in the *Chronicle* article was a stack of one-hundred-dollar bills so new the corners could cut. Tucker counted out the bills three times. He spread two thousand dollars out on his bed, more money than he had ever seen at one time. The Cajun King had joined the Tucker Davis Campaign. Tucker placed the money from his newest friend into the envelope and put it in the inside pocket of his double-breasted suit.

"Who was the package from?" Mrs. Davis asked.

Tucker grabbed the car keys on the dining table. "The Governor," Tucker said skipping out the door as the phone rang.

"Is Tucker there?"

"I'm going to need you to swing by and get me since Tucker just took my car keys," Mrs. Davis said into the phone.

"Go grab the keys," Dr. Davis said into the other end of the phone line.

"What's wrong?"

"He's in the Austin paper. You remember Stephenson in Austin, fellow philosophy chairman at the university? He just called to congratulate me because he had read an article about school board candidate Tucker Davis taking on the special interests in the paper."

"Well, that is great dear. Tell him we say thank you."

"*What*?" Dr. Davis mumbled, all too familiar with which side proffered the fool's elixir of encouragement and dementia to his son. "It means the story of our unstable son is being syndicated. This story has escaped outside of Houston!"

Dr. Davis sought out the sudden silence on the other end. "What is it?"

"You are not going to want to hear this now," Mrs. Davis said. "But Tucker did just say he got a letter from the governor."

"A letter about what? From the governor of Texas?"

"I think he meant the *other* governor."

— - — - —

"He ain't crazy, he's mad!" the crowd chanted in the Memorial Independent School District administration building.

Tucker stood between the chanting crowd and the seven school board members in the bronze suit of his candidacy announcement. The school board members sat behind a long, elevated congressional-committee-type table with eight microphones, a vacant seat where the superintendent would have sat. Behind the table, Walker's eyes followed the fedora climb and kamikaze dive in the air, a baton conducting the various rabble. It felt like he was two feet off the third base bag and coaching again, helplessly watching as Tucker paced the baseball dugout and rallied his team against him. In two minutes the meeting would commence and he would take control, Walker reassured himself.

"He ain't crazy, he's mad!"

There were students. More students in the first few rows than Walker had ever seen at a school board meeting, and they chanted as if it were a baseball playoff pep rally. Loudest of all was a large contingent of senior citizens who formed an angry swirling mob in the middle rows. People Walker's age lined the walls of the room, many holding fliers and with faces that seemed to Walker to condone the madness by the two other age demographics in the room. On the far right front row with one leg crossed over the other was Fisher, the bloodhound hiding behind his long poker face and doubtlessly enjoying the now biweekly ritual of Tucker humiliating Walker. In front of Walker, the school district secretary dumped a tower of blue forms filled out by citizens wishing to speak during the Citizens Participation portion of the meeting.

One week ago to the day it was Walker B. Moore Day. Walker's day off was getting worse. No one was supposed to come to a school board meeting. That was the point. You voted and elected the candidate you trusted, and he or she did what was best for the school district with the assistance of the superintendent in the monthly meeting. Walker had not run for election and won to preside over a mob. In his six years on the school board, there had never been a meeting where the audience filled more than half of the room. The mundane Memorial Independent School District meetings were an example of an efficient bureaucracy run by a trusted few. Walker needed to have a talk with Superintendent Marshall regarding the destructive force of Tucker Davis. Walker would not permit another mutiny led by Tucker.

"He ain't crazy, he's mad!"

Assembled before the school board was chaos. Walker knew it was not a business model to be duplicated. Did the assembled really wish for their imbalanced conductor to run things on the school board? Tucker would never stick to the agenda.

"He ain't crazy, he's mad!"

He's crazy, he's mad, and he's not coachable, Walker chanted to himself, adjusting the chant to suit the rival candidate as he adjusted his microphone. Who were these people and where did they find the zeal in their chant? It was like pirates had raided a retirement home and presented the occupants with the choice of either becoming active in school board politics or walking the plank. Certainly, the students needed to be at the baseball game in less than an hour cheering on their team with this wasted enthusiasm, and so did Walker. Walker saw they were being led by his opponent to drink from a poisoned well.

"Here! Here!" Walker's voice pounded the microphone for order. He straightened up his athletic frame. "All stand for the pledge of allegiance."

The pledge recited, and Tucker seated in the front row, Walker read an opening statement about the superintendent's visit to meet the governor and read the agenda for the meeting.

Walker looked up from the statement to address the crowd. "As President of the Board, I wish to note there is no legal requirement that the public be given the opportunity to speak at Board meetings, though it is the wish of the Board to hear from district citizens at the end during the Citizens Participation portion. Please refrain from disturbances until then."

Tucker sprung from his seat and said to the crowd, "No illegal comments disagreeing with the Board and Memorial National, y'all."

The crowd erupted in comments. "Tell him, Catfish!" "We came here to be heard!" "This isn't a democracy!"

"Disturbances such as those," Walker said, resuming with the agenda.

The agenda: recognition and plaques for the April 1999 MISD Employee and Volunteer of the Month; a vote by the Board for adoption of new monthly facility improvement status reports; a request placed by one board member for an extra week of class (to boos from the students); an announcement of the purchase of thirty acres in north Spring Branch for future construction; and review of a proposed consulting contract with Energy Education Incorporated.

The agenda covered, Walker looked at the clock. Fifteen minutes until the first pitch. The school district secretary placed the microphone and stand in the middle of the aisle in the first row. With great reluctance, Walker reached for the top blue form and called the first name.

Her black pin-striped suit was tailored. It fit the lady snuggly but did not constrict her as she walked up to the microphone. She pulled what Walker recognized as Fisher's article in yesterday's paper from her portfolio.

"Is the Board aware," the lady asked, "that not only will the passage of the Memorial TIRZ have the inverse effect of lowering the value of homes in Memorial by increasing the commercial development and activity in our neighborhood, but that the appointed Memorial TIRZ Board, whoever it is, will be granted the authority to widen roads, add extensions, and build over detention drainage, making our homes even more susceptible to flooding? The state statute I hold in my hand here reads, 'A Tax Incremental Reinvestment Zone is for areas of blight . . .'"

Tucker led the crowd in giving the lady a standing ovation when Walker notified the lady her four minutes were up. "Every kid a king!"

"Every kid a king!" the crowd echoed. "Every kid a king!"

Walker sorted through the pile discreetly as they cheered his downfall. He did not want to appear he was cherry-picking issues. In keeping with his recent fortune, all forms listed the subject as the Memorial TIRZ. He scanned the forms and skipped several with the name Tucker Davis. One name jumped at Walker. Steal a page from Tucker Davis, advised the psyche of Walker Moore. Rope it in, lighten the tension, divert the mob, roll the dice and make a circus out of it, and change the course of the game. Tacking, Walker called upon his mock game-announcer voice to inject a little humor into the room and said, "Up next, the Silver Fox."

A splitting clamor—not the sweet sound of bemusement Walker expected from voicing such a preposterous name—went up the middle of the room from the gallery of old people, to a degree, Walker was sure, was not healthy for senior citizens. Was that the pitch of old people laughing? The cultish, fox-in-the-henhouse handshake Tucker gave the old man in blue pants and white shirt with slick-backed grey hair and a suntan matching Tucker's suit told Walker his psyche was not to be trusted again. This Silver Fox of the blue form motioned for the entire room to rise for Citizens Participation.

"Do you see these people, Mr. President?" the Silver Fox asked.

Walker nodded.

"I want the whole school board to take a look at the good people of Shady Oaks."

The school board members looked at the crowd and each other and nodded.

"We might not have the money to bribe you like Memorial National," the Silver Fox said. "We might not even have a home in the fall if you pass the Memorial TIRZ. But we are going to vote out each and every one of you scoundrels and make sure none of you ever run in this city for anything ever again." He turned to the school district secretary who hurriedly typed and said, "Put that in the minutes, name's Silver Fox."

It was several minutes before the crowd stopped cheering and sat down.

"There have been no bribes taken, sir," a school board member said, a tiny bespectacled man in his late fifties at the end of the table. "Tonight has brought to our attention that a review is in order of the merits of the Memorial TIRZ for the citizens of our school district. I ask, President Moore, that we put in a request to initiate a review of the Memorial TIRZ."

"Agreed," Walker agreed unwillingly, hoping for a way out to the baseball game now that his fellow school board member was on record abandoning him. "There are ten minutes remaining of the Citizens Participation portion. I apologize to the rest of the Board and the citizens here tonight, but I must excuse myself from the current meeting. I will turn over the proceedings to the Board Vice President."

"Why won't you debate this kid?" the Silver Fox challenged Walker before he could stand up and exit.

"Excuse me? Your four minutes are up, sir," Walker said. Tucker put his hand on the shoulder of the Silver Fox to tag in. "There is a scheduled debate next week. I encourage you all to attend and ask the candidates questions then."

"You promise not to leave the debate early if we attend?" Tucker asked.

The crowd laughed at Walker who had not selected any of Tucker's twenty blue forms for this reason. Tucker clenched his fists in front of his waist and pushed them down to his knees and threw them up unclenched in the air, miming igniting a dynamite box and explosion.

"My son has a baseball game tonight," Walker pleaded with the crowd who dropped donations in a tan fedora being passed around the room. Walker exited to a chorus of boos that rode him all game.

Five

Carlos watched Tucker sop his sliced beef sandwich in warm sauce and, with three bites—two bites while still in line waiting to get rung up by the cashier—swallow it all. Under the coarse fur of the buffalo head mounted on the wall, Tucker raised his small white bowl of leftover barbeque sauce and addressed the restaurant patrons. He ceremoniously drank it over the protestations of the restaurant owner and customers and pronounced firmly, in the capital of East Texas, "That is finer than any West Texas barbeque sauce I've ever tasted." Elliott snapped a Polaroid picture and Tucker signed it for the owner and suggested it would fit well alongside the restaurant's framed pictures of fellow outlaw politicians Billy the Kid and Jesse James.

"Tuck Davis, school board," Tucker said, handing the owner an additional bright yellow paper flier and promising him a campaign sign for his restaurant once they received them later in the week. In black ink, the flier had a picture of Walker Moore with a headline below asking, "What Is Moore Yellow, Our School Board President or This Flier?"

"Where did those clouds all go?" Elliott pulled his stuck shirt off his chest outside the restaurant. "How do you wear that suit in this humidity? The sun is cooking us today."

"Slow cooked, like tender East Texas brisket," Tucker said.

"The temperature is supposed to break a Houston record this afternoon," Duna said.

"We could go hang out by my pool," Elliott said. "An in-service day is meant to be a holiday."

"Have you lost your mind, Elliott? This is the perfect opportunity to campaign," Tucker said. "There's no school."

"Swimming doesn't sound like such a bad idea. I recommend that you increase the number of in-service days if elected for such activity," Carlos said, hoping Tucker might take the hint.

"I just might have to do that," Tucker said. "It would give a student candidate for school board a chance to campaign on a school day and a fair shake at this."

"Do you want to campaign here along the shopping strips of Long Point Road or continue like before lunch, going door to door in the Spring Branch neighborhoods and introducing yourself?" Duna asked.

"I liked your idea during lunch, Duna, of staying here on this road and shaking some hands," Tucker said. "Look at that whole group of guys just standing around over on the corner!"

Cars skidded on the asphalt as horns blared. The group Tucker had spotted was a group of twenty Hispanic men. They waited around on a corner to be offered work, Carlos was about to explain to Tucker, before Tucker galloped across the street in front of oncoming cars in both directions. Two of the men jumped in the back of a pickup with construction equipment as Tucker reached the group.

"Y'all are going to miss my speech," Tucker yelled at the two Hispanics in the back of the truck pulling away. "I guess one of y'all will have to fill in your friends later on about what I have to say." Tucker walked over, hat in hand, to the oldest man who wore a cowboy hat. "Here's the deal."

Carlos listened as Tucker ranted, raved, and waved his hands for five minutes to the Hispanic crowd whose silence Tucker mistook for devotion. Carlos did not mistake their blank stares as they looked at the fliers they were unable to read.

"That's Walker Moore and the Memorial TIRZ for y'all," Tucker said. Finished speaking, Tucker traded the straw cowboy hat of the oldest Hispanic back for his fedora, each having worn the other's hat while Tucker was speaking. Carlos construed this hat swap as another mistaken cultural custom Tucker believed in honoring. "Who of y'all stands with me?"

The eldest in the cowboy hat gathered with the two other oldest men and spoke to Carlos in Spanish. The group told Carlos they were confused what work the gringo offered.

"Y'all can talk to me," Tucker reassured the group of Hispanics. "Believe me, I'm a friend of the working man just like Carlos."

"What is your story? What are you offering? Who are you?" Duna translated for Tucker.

"You speak Spanish, Duna?" Carlos asked.

"Of course she does," Tucker said, smiling at Duna. "There's nothing this prom date of mine can't do. Hell, she could write the meanest press release you've ever seen in Spanish."

"After three years of studying it," Duna replied, "I hope I can speak it."

"That hasn't helped our candidate here, who's been studying it since the seventh grade," Elliott said.

"What's my story? Dammit," Tucker said, "I was sure as hell we were getting my story out there." Tucker promised the group of Hispanics, "I aim to fix this and get my story out there. Hell, Davy Crockett published an autobiography before he ran for Congress."

At the mention of the famous Alamo participant who purportedly killed hundreds of Mexican soldiers single-handedly before his death, the group of Hispanics stirred and, in a low rumble, spoke to each other. The eldest in the cowboy hat pulled Carlos aside and repeated the question and asked about the veiled threat of Tucker's Alamo allusion.

"They want to know what jobs you can offer. That's why they wait here," Carlos said to Tucker.

"Like the Kingfish, Catfish can get you a job on the payroll if elected," Tucker said to the man in the cowboy hat. "I understand waiting around out here for work. Don't you think I know how long you have waited for jobs? Walker Moore sure doesn't know about waiting, that I can offer up to you. That's why I need your support and votes in two weeks."

"They are illegals," Carlos said.

"Illegal aliens," Elliott translated. "They cannot vote."

"Can't *vote*?" Tucker asked. "Well, we can't have that. Get their names, and we'll follow up with them to see they all get registered. There's a way to squeeze them on the voting rolls."

The group of Hispanics protested the effort by Carlos to round up their names on the petition against the Memorial TIRZ. "They want work, not trouble," Carlos translated.

"If I hear your story correctly, it's the same story of a lot of little folks in this district," Tucker said to the crowd. He took off his hat and said to the eldest in the cowboy hat, "You put your name down on that and I will pay each one of these men of yours fifty dollars to put fliers in the mailboxes in the Spring Branch neighborhoods with us."

"That's half the money Governor Boudreaux donated," Elliott said.

"If that's what it takes, then we'll just have to raise more money," Tucker said. "I reckon the Governor gave us cash so we wouldn't count it too closely for campaign expenses."

"It's illegal, Tuck, to falsify accounting records for a political campaign," Elliott said.

"*Accounting* practices? We ain't talking about running a damn company. We're merely factoring in future donations that will account for this," Tucker said. "Hell, I even thought of an idea earlier where we could filter money from Lagniappe Valet Parking gigs."

Carlos translated the terms of the deal Tucker offered. The old man took off his cowboy hat, smiled, and spoke to Carlos and Duna. "They accept," Carlos said.

Tucker met the old man's hand and nodded in the direction of Elliott, Carlos, and Duna, rolling his eyes and addressing the misunderstanding with the one word of Spanish in his vocabulary, "*Niños.*" Tucker led the group of men to the back of Elliott's pickup truck and passed out one hundred fliers to each person who signed the petition, laughing with them about the innocent kids on his campaign team who were too green to follow their political negotiations.

"Can I talk to you a moment, as one of your campaign managers?" Carlos asked Tucker. "This isn't going to look good when people see you have hired illegals to campaign for you. If President Moore gets wind of this information, he'll use it against you in the press." Carlos knew Tucker would not hesitate to do the same thing if the roles were reversed.

"Ortega, you and me come from the same stock it sounds like," Tucker said grinning. "Well, except for the fact that I never got fired from a job." Tucker gathered the group of Hispanic males and said, "If people start asking about who paid y'all to pass out these fliers, lie and say y'all can't speak English."

"*Comprendo*," the group answered.

— - — - —

The entrance to the River Oaks Country Club was at the end of the expansive River Oaks Boulevard, an esplanade lined with the oaks and dream houses that had made the 1920s planned community the most famous and expensive neighborhood in the city. A Texas ranch house next to an English Tudor; a Versailles Palace variation next to a Southern Plantation suited for a plantation the size of modern Houston. The palaces of River Oaks were built after World War I by the new kings in the Age of Oil. During the war, the location housed and trained soldiers as Camp Logan, and the planned memorial to the soldiers of that war became the monument of River Oaks, and with what remained, Memorial Park.

From the dining room of the River Oaks Country Club, Walker faced the golf course and chipped at the crust of his crème brulee with his spoon. Walker loved to position himself to face the rolling fairway of the eighteenth hole as it emerged like the humps of a sea monster from the Buffalo Bayou wood line. On the banks of the bayou, rust-colored sycamore trees leaned over a hundred feet tall, ensnared by jungle vegetation and willow trees bordering golf course and bayou. Balls lost, plunked below to murky waters, the current pushing and low waters revealing the white tops in the sand like lost pearls. His retreat cut off by the Synergy CEO and the chief operations officer at the table, Walker imagined finding pearls again on the sandy bayou banks.

"Not bad for the son of a Baptist preacher off the Missouri farm," the CEO said, concluding his meal with the same line he had used after each meal since being admitted as a River Oaks Country Club member last year.

"Not bad at all," the chief operations officer said, who owned a home nearby but remained on the membership waiting list. "Some of us have to pull ourselves up by our bootstraps and learn to eat other people's lunch to one day earn the right to eat lunch here. We can't all be one of the Moores of Houston."

Lost among the pearls to be found outside the window, Walker said, "I remember when my grandfather donated a stretch of land along the bayou to the country club so it could expand. We used to swim and search for golf balls there as kids."

"What happened last night at the administration building, Walker? It's all over the paper again," the CEO said. "I thought I was reading about Mardi Gras."

"We're hiring you a campaign manager," the chief operations officer said.

"I don't need a campaign manager," Walker said. "I beat my last opponent more than two to one—and he wasn't a kid."

"The deal's off with Sundance Oil & Gas," the chief operations officer said.

"*What?*"

"It's off."

"What are you talking about? I personally negotiated an exclusive deal with Sundance Oil & Gas at this table," Walker said knocking on the table. "I introduced Donovan Kirby to the new group at the Synergy International Conference."

"That was then. That's why we didn't have you put *us* in an exclusive deal with them. We wanted to hedge our bets."

"This was the first quarter our stock price went down in six years," the CEO said.

"Only one and a half percent lower, which is bound to happen at some point over the course of six years. Last week at the conference you said you expected the stock to jump to one hundred twenty-six dollars a share next quarter," Walker said to the chief operations officer.

The chief operations officer held up crossed fingers. "I hope to give our shareholders an even better return."

"Not by welshing on our verbal agreement and backing out of a major deal at the last minute," Walker said.

"Wall Street thinks we have too many irons in the fire. We don't need another sprawling oil and gas pipeline company weighing us down."

"He's right, Walker," the CEO said, rubbing the bald hump in the middle of his head. "We've got to focus on the future and the next big thing. This isn't the same energy business we came up in. Playing hardball doesn't always mean pulling the trigger. It also means not pulling the trigger on a deal."

"Sundance Oil & Gas is a hard asset," Walker said. "We can't trade in the volume we do without some pipelines providing cash flow and revenue. All Sundance does is make money."

"The company would make money slowly and over time," the chief operations officer said. "But you need to think outside the box." The chief operations officer unfurled the unused white napkin next to him. "'In the white space,' as we used to say in consulting."

Walker had discovered hardball at the River Oaks Country Club, though it had been with a slung golf ball on the bayou bank with his cousin. He played against a pungent brown and black banded water moccasin that hissed at him, and was clearly not a member. Walker had stepped up and flung the ball and nailed the triangle head. Surprising himself with his courage, Walker only turned tail when the territorial snake gave chase.

"I don't drive the open-top jeep that you race in annual international off-road desert competitions. And I did grow up in a different energy business than you did," Walker said to the chief operations officer. "I might be the Last Wildcatter. But I can still play hardball. Play it all the way to the bone if necessary."

The CEO and chief operations officer congratulated their white knight, mounted back in the stirrups. "Let's go hit a bucket of balls," the CEO said.

— - — - —

Candy Boudreaux applauded beside her husband as he defied the gag order and spoke to the crowd of reporters and supporters outside the courthouse.

"People are always asking me, 'Governor, who is your heir? What man of the people will look after the little folks after you are gone?' I stand here today on these courthouse steps not to proclaim how I have been falsely accused in yet another government witch-hunt or to defy the judge's gag order on the trial, but to tell you, there is another," Bobby said. "He does exist. And he reminds me so much of myself that I feel as if he were my own son."

Fat, bald, impatient, and with all the entitlement of the father without any of the talent or charm, the son, also on trial for racketeering and extortion, rolled his eyes and wore his permanent, unchanged sneer as his father spoke over the gag order. The oldest of the Boudreaux children, the son was almost twice the age of Candy, whose brainchild this new approach had been. Bobby averted the eyes of his natural son to stay with the image of his newly adopted one. The reporters pushed closer and the boom microphones dipped toward Bobby. Bobby leaned forward and accepted the familiar, loving embrace.

"It is with a great and warm feeling in my heart that I tell you there will be someone else to carry on the fight, the light of the people," Bobby Boudreaux said. "And may the bright light shine on Tucker Davis, an eighteen-year-old senior in high school and a candidate for school board. You can call him Catfish, because he's one of us. The odds are long that Catfish can beat the incumbent president of the school board and the real corruption behind the machine politics that put the president in power, but there is nothing but fight in this kid who believes every kid should be a king. He hails from Houston, our sister city on the Gulf Coast, and I encourage you all to donate and support and pray for this courageous kid of the people. I will continue to keep in correspondence with Tucker, who began writing me to keep my head up during the trial as he and most others have known of my innocence throughout this tragic ordeal, and I will be mailing a check to his campaign later today. A political disciple of our own Huey and Earl Long, Tucker Davis is a tribute to the great state of Louisiana and the great people that make our state the most unique in the country. He might be the last chance we have at representing that great tradition. God bless Catfish and his crusade to fight for the justice of the little man."

Candy, Bobby, his son, and their lawyer climbed in the limousine. "Didn't you already send Tucker a check?" Candy asked.

"Sent him two grand in cash from the penny bank fund to grease the tracks," Bobby said.

"That is a lot of pennies," the lawyer said.

"And you want to throw away more money on this ridiculous kid?" the son asked.

"The check will be something he can hold up to the press with my name on it," Bobby said. "That will be worth every penny."

— - — - —

At the end of the form, in the signature block, a stick-on red plastic arrow said, "Sign here." Dr. Green read again through the file and the consulting plan that proposed to save the district hundreds of millions of dollars in energy bills. The cornerstone of the energy usage reduction plan was conservation; turning off the lights when teachers left the classroom was the third-ranked suggestion.

Attached to the top of the folder was a handwritten reminder by Dr. Marshall that all other head principals had signed in the recommendation block. The money saved, he stated, would allow the district to build a student art center. Reading through the file a third time, Dr. Green reaffirmed her initial conclusion. The plan was worthless to the district, perhaps heinous, at the cost of fifty-two million dollars. She would type her recommendation for rejection and hand it to Mrs. Bryce to send back to Dr. Marshall. What had all her colleagues seen in the plan to recommend it? She looked at the name of the company again. Energy Education Incorporated. Dr. Green mentally noted never to invest in the company.

Dr. Green returned to reading the *Chronicle* article, relieved she had not been at the administration building last night. Dr. Green read the report about the senior citizens' participation and wondered how Tucker convinced hundreds of old people to support him. People Tucker's own age did not listen to him.

— - — - —

"The story of Tuck Catfish Davis is the story of a sacker." Tucker was writing on unlined drawing paper at his desk under the eyes of the Kingfish on the wall above him.

If, as my family always tells folks, my poor mother gave birth to an alligator, it was during the summer of my sixteenth year that I started sacking and became "Catfish." I suppose I could spin y'all a few yarns about fights and my ring-tailed roarer years before sacking, but most of it would put a standing grizzly bear to sleep. The only thing worth noting is that I was weaned on the tales of Louisiana Governor Huey P. Long, his younger brother Governor Earl K. Long, and Governor Bobby Boudreaux. My late Uncle Remy claimed to have personally known Governor Earl and even did ole' crazy Earl a favor or two at the end of Earl's life. That's why Earl gave him his hat, which my Uncle Remy later gave to me. So I reckon you could say it was a natural fit to end up going into politics as a populist one day, I just didn't know I would be the last.

But there I go again, sidetracked on politics. This is a story about sacking and my summer sacking began with an interview with store manager, Mr. Honeycutt, the Duke of Directives, a new rule every day by the ruler. He was as slick as a river's muddy bottom, but he didn't account for hiring a catfish that swam in the stuff and soon turned his store employees against him. I don't honestly recall sacking a whole lot that summer, but I sure remember the conversations I had with the good workers, trying to get them to get behind me and turn on the bosses in office. And what follows is the story of a sacker and the little folks of that store, folks like you and me, who gave name to a kid they would call Catfish.

"That ain't half bad for a first chapter," the author of *Every Kid A King* said to the other author in the room, Huey P. Long, author of *Every Man A King*. "Got to dynamite Walker Moore and keep him bleeding."

Tucker wrote a note to review chapter one for grammatical mistakes. Duna had proofread and revised the campaign press release he had assigned her ten times before sending it to Fisher Hughes. Writing impressed Duna the way politics did Tucker. If only he could write the way he politicked, it would not be such a battle to win Duna over. Tucker glanced up at Huey above his desk and caught sight of Duna's press release on top of one of the stacks of biographies. "Governor," Tucker said showing him the press release, "my pretty little stubborn mule prom date packed this with enough powder and fire to burn through two wet mares. You might say she chopped old Walker Moore down to frying size with her pen."

— - — - —

"Your article is without punch. I read it twice and still don't understand anything about this illegal immigration bill protest at the Galleria," the editor said, bouncing a tennis ball behind his office desk. Above his desk, a calendar counted down to the coming Y2K apocalypse.

"I must say, the protest lacked fight," Fisher said. He could not help but think that the one thing the protest was lacking was a populist to lead it. A Cesar Chavez. A Tucker Davis. A believer. Tucker was part believer, part snake-oil salesman in a travelling medicine show, fighting an enemy of his imagination, and an issue courtesy of Fisher's imagination. The school board meeting had been more of a revival led by Tucker than a political demonstration.

"Rewrite it."

"I just might have a substitute, chief," Fisher said. Fisher passed him the new Tucker Davis campaign press release. "A very interesting read on campaign contributions."

"The Memorial TIRZ dog is done playing fetch. Your school board meeting article was a good encore."

"I thought the same thing, but I didn't know about the sums in there."

The editor put on his bifocals and read the press release.

The school board campaign of Tucker Davis has accepted zero dollars from corporations and has received no indirect support from political action committees funded by soft money. So why is it that School Board President Walker Moore has accepted over $14,000 from Memorial National over the past six years? We also now know why Mayor Whiting voted in favor of creating a Memorial TIRZ: $68,000 sure helps swing things. As for the shepherd of the bill, City Councilman Skip Brammer accepted $38,525 from Memorial National employees during his last campaign, or more than half of his total campaign contributions. The campaign to elect Tucker Davis to Memorial Independent School District school board *seat number five proposes: VOTE OUT THIS CORRUPTION AND ENCOURAGE WALKER MOORE TO QUIT ANOTHER CAMPAIGN.*

"Brammer received over thirty-eight thousand dollars from Memorial National?" the editor asked.

"My old classmate."

"I thought Walker Moore was your old classmate."

"He was, too. In fact, Skip and Walker used to be thick as thieves."

"It appears the two still are thieves. Look into these statements. You can print the illegal immigration protest article as is. Did you come across these sums when you were writing the Memorial TIRZ article last week?"

"I guess I should have dug a little deeper."

The editor tossed the tennis ball at Fisher, who caught it. "Stop allowing these kids to do your job for you unless you want to be replaced by the damn internet. Get your shovel and go dig. And not just with this school board race, but find out what is going on underground at city hall. Uncover something. Let's run it in tomorrow's edition."

Six

Tucker bypassed the erasers swollen with chalk in Mrs. Bridge's classroom. He wiped the chalk dust off the Most Outstanding Teacher of the Year plaque resting in the tray of the blackboard and said to Mrs. Bridge, "You should hang this up. I didn't get you this award for it to gather dust."

Mrs. Bridge stayed planted in her chair. "You have the lowest average in my class, your last paper was late and only two pages long—comparing Huey Long's first race for Railroad Commissioner to the chasing of the white whale—and now you want my endorsement?"

"The endorsement of the teachers' union, yes."

Tea spilled down the side of Mrs. Bridge's chin and onto her blouse. "You want the union's endorsement also?"

"Preferably both," Tucker said. He grabbed the plaque and sat down on the other side of Mrs. Bridge's desk. Tucker, wanting to invoke a fond memory to leverage his present cause, presented the plaque again to Mrs. Bridge. He set it down on her desk next to her cup of tea when she did not move to take the offering. "If I can get you to personally sign off as well, I would be much obliged. But I need you as the representative of the union to vouch for my character in this race so I can lock up the endorsement. I believe it is vital to my campaign, as it would erase any doubts regarding my lack of educational experience."

"Who cares about the endorsement? What about the fact you might have to repeat your senior year of high school?"

Tucker mulled over this novel idea by the Most Outstanding Teacher of the Year. The Kingfish had been expelled, but Tucker could not remember if Uncle Earl or Governor Boudreaux did an extra postgraduate year. "You're right, I probably don't want to repeat my senior year," Tucker said. "However, an extra year here would shore up my problem of a lack of educational experience. And I could get a lot accomplished if I had an extra year in office as senior class president."

"You do not want to fail your senior year, Tucker. It would hurt you," Mrs. Bridge said, "politically."

Tucker smiled. "You are right again. This is why we attached 'outstanding' to your name." Tucker was impressed again by the counsel of the teacher who always wrote notes at the end of his papers longer than the paper itself. "This is my year, this is my race. This is the time—not next year—to take back our district, students and teachers together. School board, Mrs. Bridge. I'm more than willing to accompany you to the next union meeting and give y'all a speech and try and sell y'all on Tuck Davis."

"You now refer to yourself in the third person?"

"I reckon you know best that grammar isn't exactly my strong suit, but who has been a better friend over the years to the teachers of this school than me, I ask you rhetorically, Mrs. Bridge? I chopped down a cherry tree to get you that plaque there, and you deserve it. I'll chop down two more to make you a plaque twice that size if you get me the union endorsement."

"Do you know that I am meeting with your parents tomorrow?" Mrs. Bridge asked Tucker, who was swinging his hands in the air, chopping down trees for wooden plaques.

Tucker stopped chopping. "I know."

"They are concerned about your grades and deteriorating English skills."

"You can't let them ground me. It would affect this campaign." If his parents grounded him, Tucker knew, it would set his campaign back weeks. Weeks he did not have to lose. Tucker pulled out a paper from a folder for Mrs. Bridge. "I thought I'd have you take a look at the first chapter, since you are an English teacher and all. I want to revise it until it is perfect and even you would be impressed with the grammar."

"You need to start worrying about yourself, Tucker, and not worry about fighting for people politically. What are you going to do when all your classmates and friends go off to college except for you?"

"I don't actually know," Tucker said. "Maybe find an open congressional seat and run."

"'You may all go to hell, and I will go to Texas,'" Mrs. Bridge read the epigraph below the title: *Every Kid A King: The Story of Sacker Catfish Davis*.

The same redness washed over the face of Mrs. Bridge that Tucker had introduced at Senior Awards Night when he exhorted her to speak. "Those words there are Davy Crockett's words," Tucker said.

"But you are already in Texas."

"Exactly."

— - — - —

Fisher waited for Mayor Whiting to cut the yellow ribbon for the new wing of the Veterans Administration Hospital. Just south of Hermann Park, the Veterans Administration Hospital was the southern end of the Texas Medical Center, a city within the city of Houston. Fisher had arrived late after getting lost several times navigating blocks of hospitals and medical research centers searching for the right tower, trailing the wrong white lab coat.

The wing was being named after a Medal of Honor recipient. Fisher listened to the mayor read the citation detailing the valor of the fallen twenty-three-year-old Marine. The location of the firefight mentioned in the award citation was a hostile village north of where he had spent part of his second rotation with his thirty-six man infantry platoon. Fisher's platoon had been lucky never to take enemy fire when they passed through on convoys heading north.

Each passing year added to the surreal murkiness of his Vietnam experience. The feeling more and more that it never really happened, when he contemplated how the hell he was a Marine and served two tours in the infantry in Vietnam and yet managed to get lost almost weekly outside a two-block radius of his apartment in the Heights. His platoon had called him Trust Fund at first, then Swamp Fox. Swamp Fox stuck after a mission when, walking point, Fisher navigated the platoon down a deep jungle draw, cutting through heavy bush for seven hours and expending their water supply, only to break through on the same side where the platoon had entered. Fisher endured the teasing from the platoon good-naturedly the rest of his time in country, grateful to have avoided a fragging.

Trying to not forget it all, Fisher stayed in the fight. But that was taxing too—the fight to remember what it was really like and convince himself how it had really occurred. He imagined another life lived, but one involving long marches, lost, on feet rotting in jungle boots, packaged food eaten in a hurry and served in a heat made worse by slapping rain down in the prone, and boredom relieved only by periods of more intense boredom. An imagined life, though not a very fun life. And a life in which his own imagination refused to cast him in as a hero despite his best efforts to manipulate the memories. For the second tour, Fisher had tried to learn how to speak Vietnamese. He acquired enough Vietnamese to offend the villagers with his military-heavy vocabulary and rough inflexion, eventually resigning himself in his last few months in country to memorizing Vietnamese words and passing notes back and forth in the village.

Mayor Whiting posed for a photograph with an older man in a VFW hat and a Silver Star on his suit lapel. A veteran of World War II, the older man was a card-carrying member of the hero generation. Fisher and his platoonmates volunteered to chase it in Vietnam a generation later, but only found each other at the end of the chase. Awarded a Silver Star for an enemy engagement at the end of his first Vietnam rotation in which he distinguished himself by being confused enough on the battlefield to appear courageous, Fisher never took it out of the little blue box the Department of the Navy sent him. Fisher stalked the mayor and his chief of staff and the three policemen in plainclothes until they were finished with the ceremony and moved out down the hospital hall.

"Mayor Whiting, can I have a minute of your time?"

"For my favorite muckraking reporter Fisher Hughes, sure. I hope you didn't come here to soil this hospital and the brave men who paid in blood for it. Shouldn't you be writing about that basket case Grail Knight of yours running for student government?"

"I was going to ask if you had any comments about my article this morning highlighting the enormous amount of money Memorial National has donated to your campaign and to some of the city council members."

"When you are mayor of a city, Mr. Hughes, you don't have time to read the papers. You should try it sometime instead of hiding behind a pen; see how easy it is."

Fisher put his pen up against his chin. "That is an idea," Fisher said. "If you run for reelection, it might be time I tried."

"I will be running, and I pray it is against a yellow journalist like you."

"Sixty-eight thousand dollars is no small amount from one company's employees."

"It costs millions to run for mayor in this city. I get a lot of donations from a lot of people, and I do not have the time you do to look up where each one works," Mayor Whiting said. "Try hacking out a story besides a kid running for student government."

"School board," Fisher rectified with a conviction in his voice not communicated since Vietnam.

— - — - —

"Let's play hardball," Walker said.

"The story made a fool out of me in Austin in front of our governor," Dr. Marshall barked through the phone line to Walker.

"Quite possibly our next president."

"This kid is creating a firestorm. How is it that *Louisiana* Governor Bobby Boudreaux is speaking about this student like he is the easy-going carpenter from Nazareth?"

"Only in Louisiana can a politician drop his wife of forty years and marry a blonde in her twenties and get re-elected! Boudreaux, who answered with a wink to some attractive female television reporter's question about his runoff opponent, an ex-Ku Klux Klan Grand Wizard, 'I'd like to think we are both wizards under the sheets.'"

"No one makes a fool out of me."

"Least of all a kid," Walker said, knowing the feeling all too well. Earlier by fax, Walker received a flier with his face on it being passed around the Spring Branch neighborhood. Walker was sure a kid was behind it.

"What happened at the school board meeting on Monday? Was it as undisciplined as I read in the paper?" Dr.

Marshall asked. "Who the hell is the Silver Fox?"

"There were hundreds of people there. Complete chaos. Tucker Davis brought the whole Shady Oaks retirement community out of retirement. Every time I tried to bring order, the crowd reacted as if I were trying to censor Tucker and stifle debate."

"There must be some clause I can get him suspended under. A suspension would kill his campaign."

"No one would vote for a suspended student. Not even the suspended student's parents."

"It is illegal to campaign on district property."

"It is?" Walker silently noted his violation of district policy last week when he asked the students in the government class to vote for him and the other incumbents, even if unopposed.

"It is now," Dr. Marshall said. "And we're going to catch him in the act."

— - — - —

A ball whizzed past Dr. Green's head as if fired from a gun as she entered the Jefferson High School gymnasium. The ball blindsided a small freshman, hitting him on the left side of his face as he tried to dodge five other oncoming balls from his right side.

"You're out!" Tucker screamed. He hovered over the small boy moaning on the ground and holding his face stamped red with the print of the ball.

Dr. Green signaled to the umpire in his cream-colored, double-breasted umpire suit to come out into the hallway. She would talk to the gym teacher later about why Tucker was not in mandatory gym clothes for gym class. "No politics," Dr. Green said.

"I don't think I understand what it is you're getting at, Doc."

"No politics," Dr. Green repeated to Tucker in the hallway. "You are not allowed to campaign on district property at any time."

"The debate will be on district property."

The debate was scheduled to be held in the auditorium next week. Dr. Green hesitated and said, "Besides the night of the debate."

"I guess I'm going to need to see something in writing as to what constitutes politics. I like to politick, but is that politics? I see a lot of gray area for a candidate to operate in and dodge this new rule. I ain't saying gray is bad either."

Dr. Marshall had been vague in his guidelines but the message was clear. "You will be suspended indefinitely, Tucker, if you are caught in violation of this rule against campaigning on Memorial Independent School District property," Dr. Green said.

"How long is indefinitely?"

"Indefinitely."

"I didn't want to have to drag lawyers and lawmen into this fight, but it might just come to that in the end. Saying 'no politics' is like draining the swamp Catfish Davis swims in, Doc. That ain't a fair way to fight a war."

"I don't make the rules, Tucker," Dr. Green appealed to the cream-suited umpire, "but I must enforce them. No politics."

Tucker threw his fedora on the ground. "What am I going to talk about if I can't talk about politics?"

There would be nothing, Dr. Green comforted herself. "Have you made any progress on the class legacy gift?"

Tucker picked his fedora up and dusted it off on his pant legs. "We've only got six hundred dollars left, but one idea I was tossing around was starting a Class of 1999 legal fund in support of Governor Boudreaux."

"Something actually tangible would be better. Governor Boudreaux is not even the governor of this state. A class legacy," Dr. Green said, "not a political legacy."

"Another idea someone brought up that I thought was pretty unique, and more tangible I reckon, was a bronze plaque with Governor Earl Long's face and a few engraved paragraphs on his contribution to the civil rights movement in the South for the new auditorium."

— - — - —

Walker picked a public place to play hardball in case he struck out. Located in a shopping strip at Westheimer and Gessner, Rudi Lechner's had served the same fine Austrian cuisine for thirty years. Inside was a walk in the Austrian Alps with Rudi, the proprietor, greeting guests and making a special drink with a flame if ordered. The best veal to be found in town, the Germanic idea of intentionally caging a calf was the nourishment Walker needed. There had been cows on the busy Westheimer Road ten years before, thought Walker, but they went to the stockyards and slaughter like everyone else who did not play hardball.

"Is that not the best *Wiener Schnitzel* you ever had?" Donovan asked. He chewed excitedly on a piece of veal half in his cavernous mouth, which anchored a face aflame. "You not hungry, Walker?"

Walker had no appetite for hardball; who was he kidding. Walker ordered another foreign draft beer, in foreign territory, swearing next time he would play in a 1950s diner. Once, after a baseball game in high school, Walker's father had taken him to such a diner for a burger and malted milkshake. Enjoying the moment so much, Walker confided to his dad he wanted to one day go into the oil and gas business like him. Before Walker finished describing his future plans, his father started telling him about something he called "the breaks of the game." The breaks of the game were that he was in love with another woman and leaving Walker and his mother. Unable to talk, Walker had felt a peculiar expansion in his stomach and concentrated on his table manners to keep it from swelling. Feeling the same expansion in his stomach now, Walker reset his fork to four o'clock and face up, his knife blade-side-in.

"Excuse me," Walker politely interjected into Donovan's story of the first time he ate Austrian food. "There is something about the deal I need to tell you."

"I was about to ask you," Donovan said. "So what time are we setting to sign the papers and make it official? My wife has been calling me nonstop this week about it since she gets half of my equity in the company because of the divorce."

"You are getting divorced?"

"Yeah, it fizzled out. My wife got bored with me—I guess after almost thirty years, opposites are failing to attract. Kind of depressing and embarrassing. I never cheated on her in all that time—not even during Vietnam, though we had only been together six months. I thought you knew about the divorce."

"The breaks of the game," Walker mumbled.

"What?"

Walker clasped his hands together underneath the table. "We're pulling out," Walker said. "Synergy's not going to pull the trigger on the deal. The CEO and chief operations officer have determined we can't afford the risk."

Donovan stood up and squeezed his napkin in his right hand and said, "I personally built the company you just screwed, Walker. Now I'm going to lose it to some other energy giant that won't let me run a damn thing. The first thing they will do is fire me and half the employees who have worked for me for over twenty-five years. How can you work for a company that acts like this? You go back and tell those sons of bitches they are the two most unethical people I've ever met!"

Donovan wound up and threw his napkin at Walker. Donovan came around the table and shook his fist with his finger pointed two inches from the curved tip of Walker's nose and said aloud to the restaurant, "You, Walker B. Moore, have not ended this dialogue with Donovan Kirby. My ginger ass didn't survive a year of jumping out of the sky and being shot at in Vietnam in the Special Forces to live to get dicked down by you and Synergy. You fucked with the wrong Green Beret. I don't know how yet, but I will ambush you and your company and leave you looking like a goat-fuck in my wake. You mess with the best, you die like the rest."

Walker did not notice the stares from the other diners as he folded the disheveled napkin Donovan had used for pitching practice, moved his drink to the right of his plate, placed the fork on his plate horizontally, and waited erect in his chair for the check.

— - — - —

Morning sunlight lit the office of *The Pony Express*. The office of the school paper buzzed with activity on the top floor of the history wing of the Jefferson High School campus. In the middle of the large open room were two rows of desks side by side, each with a computer. Blank white butcher paper hung from three of the four walls in the shape of a horseshoe, designated by the journalism teacher as the "Mustang Creative Zone." At Tucker's request, Duna ceased the creativity and kicked out all the staff, either working or hanging out against the walls on bean bag chairs waiting on the first morning bell. Tucker was impressed by how the students responded to Duna's command. High school students were Tucker's toughest audience.

"You won't hear a lot of compliments from me regarding politics, but your work here has been brilliant the past few weeks," Tucker said to his prom date. "And that's not from just me. Fisher Hughes said so himself."

"Tell him I need a summer internship," Duna said.

Tucker turned to Elliott and said, "Call Mr. Thibodaux at Lagniappe Valet Parking and have him create a summer internship program as a favor to me."

"Summer internship at the paper," Duna said, "in journalism."

Tucker contemplated the reach of his payroll and influence. "I can probably arrange that."

"My parents have invited you to dinner tonight at five o'clock before the talent show if you can come. They very much want to meet you since you are taking me to prom."

"I will be there."

"No politics," Duna advised.

"Speaking of no politics," Elliott said.

"I had a little meeting yesterday with Dr. Green," Tucker said.

"No politics," Elliott said. "He can't talk politics or campaign on district property."

"Why not?" Duna asked.

"Because Dr. Green will suspend him if he does."

"Why can't you campaign though?"

"Dr. Green says it's illegal and against district policy. I was looking at the district bylaws and I'm not so sure I agree with her."

"What do you intend to do?" Duna asked. "I can write an editorial in the paper against the policy."

Tucker knocked twice on the one wall not a part of the creative zone and pulled out a copy of the first chapter of *Every Kid A King* from his inner jacket pocket and smiled. "Let's serialize a chapter each week in *The Pony Express*."

"Dr. Green will suspend you," Elliott said.

"Loosen up, Elliott," Tucker said. "This falls under autobiography and not politics. I proofread it three times, Duna. What do you think?"

"It's only a page long," Duna said. "I'll have to read it first and get back to you. We did just have two seniors who were supposed to be writing articles quit last week."

"Give me until third period," Tucker said, "and I'll get you the second chapter. I'll make the next chapter a page longer for you."

"I don't know that we've done something like this before."

"Never has a student run for school board either. This redoubles our attack against Walker Moore. If y'all will excuse me, I've got a fireside chat to deliver."

"Where are you going?" Duna asked.

"To do the morning announcements," Tucker said. He stopped at the door and turned back. "Duna, you play the fiddle, right?"

"I play the violin, yes."

"I will probably have to slot you to play 'Red River Valley' at the talent show."

"No politics," Duna whispered to Elliott. "Do you think Dr. Green will suspend him if we print his story, Elliott?"

"I think that's a safe assumption," Elliott said.

"Should we stop him?"

"Can you?"

— - — - —

Fisher joined his father for a lunchtime cocktail in the clubhouse after hitting a bucket of golf balls at the Houston Country Club.

"Your mom and I have been following your articles on the Memorial TIRZ in the paper," Mr. Hughes said. He stretched his left arm behind his head with his right hand pushing down on the elbow. "As a former banker, I feel torn about it."

"You think it will pass?" Fisher asked.

"Probably," Mr. Hughes said. "Too much money and momentum behind it. Mayor Whiting doesn't usually lose."

"He needs to lose. In my opinion he has been terrible for the city."

"You're not supposed to have an opinion as the city reporter."

"Houston deserves better than the mediocrity he has brought us as mayor. It will never grow into a first-rate city," Fisher said, "without a vision."

"Growing is not one of Houston's problems. I remember Lanny Whiting when he was a first-year associate, long before he was a mayor," Mr. Hughes said. "You may be right, but who wants to be mayor? Managing a large municipality is tedious: all the city's unanswerable problems are your problems."

"Yesterday," Fisher said, "I was at the V.A. Hospital for a ribbon cutting ceremony and to interview the mayor, and the realization dawned on me that I could do it, and do it better."

Mr. Hughes laughed. "Fisher King Hughes, you have been writing too many articles about this delusional student. The delusions are starting to run in your head, son."

"Is the idea that farfetched? I used to be in politics."

"Do you mean politics as in president of your high school class?"

"A great many famous politicians got their feet wet as senior class presidents. Some even mention senior class president in their bios," Fisher said. "I've been thinking about moving on from writing about politics to throwing my hat in the ring for years. I am a Vietnam veteran."

"Look at the President in the White House—no one gives a damn about Vietnam. People would rather forget than think about it. Vietnam was not the Second World War, when people cared if you served," Mr. Hughes said. "They should give a damn about it. It was our longest war and 58,000 of your brothers did not come home. I was a Marine at Guadalcanal, so I get it. But we're a small, dying minority."

"I've been a political reporter here in Houston for over twenty years—"

"You're gay."

"And I'm gay," Fisher said. "Houston can't have a gay mayor?"

"Have you lost your mind, son? Can you imagine what your candidacy would do to your mother? She has yet to tell her side of the family you came out."

"I came out thirty years ago when I got back from Vietnam," Fisher said. "Am I supposed to wait another thirty years? I joined the Marine Corps because I knew how disappointed you would be when I told you I was gay. Things have changed, Dad. It's not an albatross anymore."

Mr. Hughes stretched his arms out in front of his chest. "Never in a million years could you get elected down here as a gay mayor. I think this new little buddy of yours running for school board is rubbing off on you, or rubbing you off."

"I'm gay, not a pedophile."

"This is still the South."

"This is Texas," Fisher said. "Houston is more the West than the South."

"It's not California either."

"I'm telling you right now, Houston would elect a gay mayor if the gay person was the most qualified person for the job. In fact, Houston will elect a gay mayor one day."

"*One day*," Mr. Hughes said. "Perhaps a hundred years from now when we stop using oil and live in space and Houston has no relevance, and this qualified gay person comes along against a competing field of unicorns. Until that day, don't be naïve. It's been almost thirty years since you told us, and your mother and I still haven't forgiven ourselves for letting you quit football your senior year."

"I haven't forgiven myself for quitting politics," Fisher said standing up. "Y'all are two votes out of two million."

— - — - —

Dr. Davis switched desks. He moved to the desk one over, leaving an empty desk between where he and his wife sat in Mrs. Bridge's classroom. Dr. Davis had not found it as amusing as Mrs. Bridge that he had by chance originally chosen his own son's desk.

"He's not failing, but he's close to failing," Mrs. Bridge said.

"Better than failing," Mrs. Davis said. "Has he shown any recent signs of improvement?"

"He did write this, which he turned in yesterday for me to look over. I could probably award him some extra credit for it. It is very creative," Mrs. Bridge said, handing over the copy of *Every Kid A King.*

Dr. Davis read the Davy Crockett quote and the first page in horror. He tried to raise both eyebrows at Mrs. Bridge, managing one successful hop of the left brow. "Creative? If you wear a coonskin cap and wrestle bears, I could see this passing for creative," Dr. Davis said. "How is he going to succeed at the university level writing and talking like a frontiersman?"

"Creative in the sense that I interpreted it to be a parody of the tall tale, a pastiche of Davy Crockett, a satire written in the American vernacular lampooning politics," Mrs. Bridge explained.

"With all due respect, you're completely wrong and I feel I must right this for you," Dr. Davis said, aghast yet another adult had fallen under the spell cast by his son that bewitched adults to read into and to seek more than was there. "Our son has no idea what a parody is, let alone irony, be it comic or tragic. He takes a book or a story at face value. All irony is lost on him, a telltale sign of mental insanity. If anything, he reads too much. This is where he drew this crazed inspiration from—from a crackpot who referred to himself as "The Kingfish." Outside of *Alice's Adventures in Wonderland*, have you ever heard of anything so fantastical? My son is *The Catfish*!"

"I think it is just 'Catfish' and not 'The Catfish,'" Mrs. Bridge said.

"He's writing a memoir about his experience as a sacker, honey," Mrs. Davis calmed her husband, whose mouth lay open wide. "That was his first job. I can't wait to read it when it's completed. I'm a librarian downtown across from city hall. Tucker used to spend all day in the library basement reading political biographies."

"You see where that has gotten us," Dr. Davis said. "Up from the basement, our son is running for school board at eighteen." Dr. Davis turned to Mrs. Bridge. "This is why it was criminal to allot two months of class time to discuss *All The King's Men*. He took the tale as a literal roadmap, which only proves my theory."

"You have more theories than anyone I know," Mrs. Davis said.

"In your estimation, do you think he needs to see a psychiatrist?" Dr. Davis asked. "A student running for school board cannot be normal from your experience, right?"

"I do not think I am qualified to say, Dr. Davis, one way or the other regarding psychiatric therapy. He is the first student I have seen run for a seat on the school board. He did, I should also disclose, ask me for my endorsement, or rather the endorsement of the teachers' union—of which I am the elected representative."

"What did you say?" Dr. Davis asked.

"A lot is going to have to change."

"Good," Dr. Davis said. He stood up and shook Mrs. Bridge's hand with both hands and said, "Thank you for telling Tucker that. A lot does need to change."

"Did Tucker say anything in response?" Mrs. Davis asked Mrs. Bridge.

"'That's all I needed to hear.'"

— - — - —

Dunazade Shari lived with her parents and younger sister in an old apartment complex between a boat storage unit and the Spring Branch Hospital in a heavily Hispanic part of town. Unfortunately for Tucker, many of the signs were in the language he had been studying unsuccessfully for six years. After a phone call from a payphone, Duna and her father met Tucker at the corner pawn shop where the owner was trying to buy Tucker's fedora. Tucker followed them to their apartment in his mother's car.

The meal of shredded spiced lamb and rice was served upon arrival. Mr. Shari apologized that they ate early each night as Duna's mother worked nights at the hospital next door. Tucker thanked Mr. and Mrs. Shari for the meal as Mrs. Shari brought in a tray of little glasses with tea and sugar at the bottom and everyone moved to the small living room. Tucker sat in a chair opposite Mr. Shari who delicately stirred the sugar with a tiny silver spoon. Tucker loosened his tie enough to slip a finger underneath, but kept his bronze double-breasted suit buttoned as Mr. Shari had not unbuttoned his suit.

"Do you know where you are going to college, Mr. Davis?" Mr. Shari asked.

"No, sir," Tucker said. He banged his spoon around in the glass trying to get the sugar to melt. "I guess I'll see how the election goes first, whether I need to stay in town or not."

"Did you apply to a lot of schools?"

"I only applied to Tulane University in Louisiana because that's where Huey P. Long did some studying. If it was a good enough school for the Kingfish, it is good enough for me. I haven't heard anything yet from the school. I might stick around here for a while and work and take some classes in Houston. You must be proud Duna got accepted to Texas."

"We would love to send Duna out of state to college but the cost is too much for our family without a scholarship," Mr. Shari said. "The University of Texas is a fine school though."

"I will have to look into getting some more scholarships for the district if I'm voted in, Mr. Shari," Tucker said. "One thing you can say about me as a politician is I'm all for giving little folks a fair shot at education."

Duna rose from the sofa. "What time do you have to be up at the school for the talent show tonight?"

"Did you get an eyelash stuck in your eye?" Tucker asked Duna, who stopped winking. "I battle the worst curvy eyelashes that blind even me occasionally."

"You are in politics, Mr. Davis?" Mr. Shari asked.

"Call me Catfish or Tuck please, Mr. Shari," Tucker said. "I am running for school board seat number five. I'm trying to take back this district of ours from these corrupt buzzards we got in there and return it back to the people. The little folks like you and me. Your daughter has been absolutely great and a huge help too."

Mr. Shari turned to Duna who played with her empty glass. "You know, Tucker, Dunazade's mother and I come from Iran originally," Mr. Shari said. "Long ago I used to be a surgeon in the state hospital, not a tailor, and she was once one of the few female lawyers in the country. We, too, have seen a movement from the people and a leader who promised the little folks, as you call them, a change from the corrupt administration. In our revolution, the leader was called Ayatollah Khomeini, and he was a charismatic speaker as well when he denounced the tyranny of the corrupt Shah."

"President Walker Moore is the *Shah* here,"Tucker said, emphasizing *Shah* to secure the two votes of Mr. and Mrs. Shari.

"Well," Mr. Shari said, "the new leader turned out to be as bad, if not worse, than the Shah. My family has personally suffered a great deal from politics in our lifetime, and that is why I am always telling Duna to stay away from it. It will only cause hardship and your hopes will be disappointed."

Tucker took another sip from the hot glass, up against another wall of no politics. Mrs. Shari set down a tray with pistachio cookies in the middle of the coffee table. The cookies sat untouched. Tucker thought about Mr. Shari's tale of the Shah and the Ayatollah.

"You must get going if you are hosting the talent show tonight," Duna said.

Tucker retrieved his hat by the table at the front door. "Then I guess Walker Moore is the Ayatollah. Because I ain't either—Shah or Ayatollah. I'm Tuck Catfish Davis, every kid a king, and I got the best prom date in the whole district. It has been a blessed honor to hear just a part of your story, Mr. Shari, this evening in your home, and I hope to hear more and learn from it. Heck, I hope you and Mrs. Shari vote for me."

Tucker straightened the fedora on his head to the formal position of wear and brought the resistant bowlegs to bear next to each other. The feet together split the knees and wobbling legs out. Tucker bent at the waist to ninety degrees. The fedora reset on his head as Tucker rose back up. It was a kowtow worthy of the Imperial Court of China, Tucker knew, from viewing a recent videotape reenactment in history class.

The sugar reformed at the bottom of Mr. Shari's glass. Mr. Shari had stopped stirring at the commencing of the Chinese kowtow in the middle of his Persian rug.

"You don't have to tell me I'm crazy to be in politics,"Tucker resumed, up from the kowtow."I got the whole world telling me the same thing. But it is who I am, just like you and Duna are Sharis. My tribe is Long, and that's why I'm the ornery fellow you had eating with you tonight. I ain't got anything else, and I reckon I don't really know anything else besides politics. I'm running for school board because if I don't, who will? I am the President of the Class of 1999 and was elected by the people of that class to fight for folks and see it through, be it a class legacy or school board. I know they've got smarter kids with more distinguished records than mine and from better families than mine, but they're usually busy charting out other things and the notion of running and serving for one reason or another just ain't there. I reckon as much that I might be wrong too, as they've got their colleges selected and I'm out here fighting for my life voluntarily and the only college I might have is school board. But I accept that and I'll see it through, even if that means I'm crazy."

Mr. Shari walked over in front of Tucker but did not take the extended hand Tucker offered. Mr. Shari stepped forward and ignored the offered hand to hug Tucker. He kissed Tucker lightly on each cheek with the respect shown between the oldest of friends and declared, "I feel like you are the foreigner, my friend. Your school board is the dream of an immigrant, not a native son. Our votes, Tucker Catfish Davis, are yours, and take my business card. Come by anytime free of charge, but please come by because your suit needs to be altered very badly."

— - — - —

Kirby Contemporary Art Gallery was a pink, two-story gingerbread house in the Montrose neighborhood just south of the bayou before downtown. It was one of three art galleries in a ten-house stretch of the street, no two adjacent houses the same pastel color. It was one of two galleries Donovan Kirby and his wife owned in Houston. The neighborhood tolerated parties well, and Joanne Kirby hosted several a week at the art gallery.

"Smells great," Donovan said to two men barbequing chicken in the front yard of the house next door to the art gallery. On each side of the art gallery lived a gay couple. Donovan never remembered their names and separated them in his head by the fact the gay couple not barbequing adopted a five-year-old boy from an orphanage in Vietnam. Donovan had no son. He liked the quiet boy who was usually playing in the front yard, though Donovan found the parents insufferable; they seemed to hold Donovan accountable as a Vietnam veteran for the boy being in an orphanage. Donovan wished to steal the boy away and journey back to Vietnam in a quest to find the boy's real parents, stopping along the way to ride elephants in the central highlands, swimming and fishing at the beaches where Donovan had relaxed on R&R, and showing the boy the old Special Forces firebase where Donovan's twelve-man Green Beret A-team, together with their partner Vietnamese Special Forces team, camped in the southern delta.

The noise from the party vibrated the glass on the front door. Donovan waded through the artists, patrons, and partygoers in search of Joanne. Dressed in an old gray suit and striped tie from his first year of law school, the looks he received made Donovan aware of the fact that none of the people in attendance knew the gray square they looked down upon was paying for the drinks in their hands.

Ex-Cotton Bowl Queen and patron of the arts, Joanne

Kirby was upstairs introducing one of her artists to another socialite couple when her husband entered and brought her up short. She excused herself from her guests to attend to Donovan.

"Donovan," Joanne said. "What on earth brings you out here?"

"We do own the gallery."

"I thought we agreed in mediation that I would keep this gallery."

"You can keep the gallery, I'm only kidding. Some party. I don't think I know five percent of the people here."

"They're not your type, my dear," Joanne said, fiddling with her ruby earrings. "A faster crowd, no military buddies. Why are you here?"

"I didn't think I had a type, except for you, my dear," Donovan said. "And I come from the *same* stale moneyed background as you, Joanne. I have consciously chosen not to associate with old money, though, as I have found they usually have so little to offer society and are rather boring with their sense of entitlement."

"Is there an end to your self-loathing?"

"Did I mention talentless, with a false sense of importance and achievement, and always telling the most tedious stories at parties?"

"Stop it, Donovan. What did you come out here for? My artists and guests expect me to make at least some effort to attend to them like a proper hostess."

"Do you think the little Vietnamese boy next door will be bullied in school because his parents are gay?" Donovan asked. "If there's one thing I've always hated in this world, it is a bully. We had a kid in the camp just like him when I was in Vietnam."

"What are you talking about?"

Donovan put his hand on Joanne's hip. "Synergy pulled out of the deal."

"How is that a binding deal if they pulled out? So what does this mean?"

"The exclusive agreement we signed wasn't binding on Synergy," Donovan said. "I'm left with trying to fend off a hostile takeover at the last minute, which will probably be worse for both of us, as you will not get as much money in the long run either."

"What do you plan to do about it?"

"Fend it off by pulling every string I can."

"I meant about the dishonest and unseemly way Walker Moore and Synergy have treated us."

Donovan smiled. "I did—in a rather grand futile gesture—make violent, empty threats to try to scare the shit out of Walker after he told me."

"Weak and hollow threats are not very becoming, Donovan. I would have thought more of you than to just roll over like this."

"What do you expect me to do about it?"

"I don't know. This is your department." Joanne waved her hand at the paintings. "I run an art gallery. You're the expert in unconventional warfare."

"That was thirty years ago against the Viet Cong," Donovan said. "Most of the war stories I've told you were lies. I had to project an image of an ex-Green Beret. Anyway, my real expertise was counterinsurgency."

"I will say we shouldn't let Walker Moore tarnish our image like this. It might set a precedent. If an eighteen-year-old boy can humiliate Walker on a weekly basis, surely larger-than-life maverick oilman Donovan Kirby can, as you used to so eloquently put it, stick the knife between the second and third rib and twist."

"What eighteen-year-old boy are you talking about?"

"The one in the news, the one the couple I was just talking to was joking about. Tucker Davis, I think his name is. The student running against Walker Moore for school board."

"School board," Donovan said. Donovan took a glass of champagne from a circling waiter's tray and grinned at his now ex-wife. The white dinner jacket and bowtie kid from the hotel terrace was the candidate for school board against Walker Moore. Unconventional warfare doctrine called for linking up with the indigenous resistance. Donovan had been trained in the Special Forces to wage unconventional warfare *by, with, and through* native allies. He had found his native ally. Tucker Davis was the white knight.

— - — - —

The twisting girl twirled a final time to the closing musical chords in the Walker B. Moore Auditorium. Dr. Green applauded in the dimming lights.

"What do you say?" Tucker asked the talent show crowd. The auditorium was more than three-quarters full and several hundred more were in attendance than had been for the Senior Awards Night and dedication. Walker and Dr. Marshall told Dr. Green they had waited in line to buy a ticket behind at least a hundred people bussed over from Shady Oaks. Onstage, Tucker entertained the crowd as host with a just-discovered-gold jig as an encore to the girl's performance studies dance number.

"Who appointed Tucker the host of the talent show?" Walker asked Dr. Green, who sat in between Walker and Dr. Marshall.

"He was voted the class clown by his classmates," Dr. Green answered feebly. In between acts was a crossfire of questioning in the darkness by Dr. Marshall and Walker. Dr. Green did not believe they had come together to take in a show in the new auditorium from the perspective of the audience. The lights came back up on a piano with Tucker standing to the side of it, his fedora hat in his hands. In the darkness onstage, a white screen lowered and a projector was set up.

"Put your hands together and welcome on piano another old friend," Tucker said to the crowd. "He's traveled down more dusty roads and ridden in more boxcars and played more ragtime than any of us kids have dreamed about. A man with hair that looks like it has been shucked from an oyster, the Silver Fox!"

"That's the guy from the school board meeting!" Walker said, reaching over Dr. Green to grab Dr. Marshall. "This is the guy, the Silver Fox. Look at all the old people cheering."

Dr. Green opened her program and discovered what she suspected. The folks from Shady Oaks were going nuts around them for an unlisted cameo by one of their own. Onstage, Tucker turned on the projector to display the lyrics to "Every Man A King" by Huey P. Long.

Dr. Marshall turned to Dr. Green and said, "I told you no politics. Handle this."

"Where is this act in the program?" Walker asked, ravaging the pages of the program for a clue.

The Silver Fox played the piano as Tucker spoke to the crowd, "All I ask is that when y'all sing the word 'man' in the song, y'all hear the word 'kid' in your hearts and sing it like your school district depends on it. Because that's the choice: Walker Moore as king, or every kid a king. Let us sing our song to ward off their scheming Memorial Tax Incremental Reinvestment Zone jinx." Tucker walked over with the microphone and pointed at the projected lyrics with his fedora and led the crowd in singing:

Why weep or slumber America
Land of brave and true
With castles and clothing and food for all
All belongs to you

Every man a king, every man a king
For you can be a millionaire

But there's something belonging to others
There's enough for all people to share
When it's sunny June and December too
Or in the Winter time or Spring
There'll be peace without end
Every neighbor a friend
With every man a king

"Ladies and gentlemen, the Silver Fox," Tucker said, walking back to the piano.

"Thank you," the Silver Fox said. He waved to the audience. "But put your hands together for Catfish, our next school board member. Vote in Tuck Davis, vote out corruption. Catfish!"

The lights faded to blackout and came back on to light an empty stage. The crowd chanted, "Catfish!"

"Is he going to bash a piñata with our faces on it for a final act?" Walker asked Dr. Green. Dr. Green stood up and turned to the aisle.

"There won't be an encore because there is no political campaigning authorized on district property. She's pulling the plug on all of this now and handling it accordingly," Dr. Marshall said to Dr. Green as the back of the auditorium erupted to the sounds of a marching band and the lights dimmed. In darkness, the Jefferson High School marching band paraded down the middle aisle to the stage playing "The Yellow Rose of Texas." People in the aisle parted to let the band through. A light came on and shone on the stage as a flute lowered from the rafters of the stage by an invisible fishing line to Tucker. Tucker grabbed the flute and used the prop to lead the band Pied Piper-like through the crowd.

Dr. Green greeted Tucker as the song ended and the lights came on in the auditorium.

"What did you think, Doc?" the fedora-wearing Pied Piper asked. "That was some show, huh?"

"You are suspended indefinitely, Tucker," Dr. Green said.

"Why?"

"You know why. No politics means no politics."

"That wasn't politics," Tucker said. "I was just teasing my opponent with a Huey Long ballad. The people loved it. You can't suspend me, Dr. Green. My parents will ground me."

"I warned you that there was to be absolutely no campaigning," Dr. Green said. "Then you throw it in my face up onstage at the talent show in front of hundreds of people."

"It was comedy," Tucker said.

"Save your speeches for your parents, who will not find their son's suspension very humorous."

"It was satire," Tucker said. "Okay, it was political satire."

Seven

Dr. Davis first answered the doorbell in his dream. When it rang a second time, he put on his tattered, once-yellow morning robe half-asleep and opened the front door of his house to three men and a delivery truck.

"Davis?" the deliverymen asked him. Dr. Davis signed, and the deliverymen carried in box after box, each the size of a refrigerator, eventually filling his study, the living room, and the family room. What products had his wife ordered off the shopping channels now? Dr. Davis tilted one of the boxes over and cut the top tape open with a kitchen knife. Finding the box light, Dr. Davis picked the bottom up and emptied the contents on the floor. His son's grinning face spilled out on the floor on yard placards and ended all hope that it was just a dream.

"Tucker!"

The commotion of the delivery and her husband's cry brought Mrs. Davis into the living room. "What is it, honey?"

Dr. Davis showed her the signs.

"How neat, he's got yard signs. That's a handsome portrait of Tucker with his hat. I'll go make some breakfast and you go wake Tucker up."

"With my boot!" Dr. Davis wondered when he would wake up from this nightmare. Suddenly the appearance of Tucker cutting between the stacks of signs and coming towards him reminded Dr. Davis of a recent political cartoon of his son in the paper that depicted Tucker with catfish features atop a human body. As a joke, Dr. Davis' colleagues had attached the cartoon to his office door and added in pencil the macabre line: WHERE'S MY HEAD?

Dr. Davis shuddered. All around him was the missing, grinning head his son had come for.

"Did you see your signs, Tucker?" Mrs. Davis asked.

Dr. Davis pushed a box blocking the door. "That would be the thirty boxes in my study, the living room, and the family room, son, delivered at six A.M."

"I got suspended."

"What?" Mrs. Davis asked. "How is that possible?"

"For campaigning at the talent show."

"Aren't you a candidate in an election? Aren't you supposed to campaign?"

Tucker sat down at the dining table. "That's what I'd figured. This administration is trying to shut me up and railroad the Memorial TIRZ through. They didn't like that Catfish was trying to make them share a little of the wealth."

"How long are you suspended?"

"You're grounded," Dr. Davis said, seizing the opportunity to reestablish parental authority.

"A few days," Tucker said. "A week. Technically indefinitely."

"What did I tell you all along about this?" Dr. Davis asked. "And now you are suspended from school. You're grounded until you are off suspension, and you will go downtown with your mother today rather than sit around here all day and cause more trouble."

— - — - —

Dr. Green bathed in the return of the quiet, stale afternoon air in her office. She knew she had not seen the last of Tucker Davis, but at least the suspension had dissipated the category-five hurricane heading straight at her school. The day had been a calm one, welcomed greedily by Dr. Green after the talent show's never-ending final act.

Mrs. Bryce knocked on her door. "Dr. Marshall is holding on line one."

"I was just calling to congratulate you on taking control of a tough situation last night," Dr. Marshall said when Dr. Green picked up the phone. "Mrs. Bryce tells me you officially suspended Tucker Davis indefinitely."

"I did."

"I would love to have seen his face. His campaign was no joke. He could have cost the school district millions of dollars."

"I monitor all the school contracts he signs as class president. He does get overcharged, but not for millions of dollars."

"I'm talking about district contracts. There will be opportunities when the Memorial TIRZ passes."

Mrs. Bryce opened the door and pointed at the front page of *The Pony Express*.

Dr. Green mumbled, "Dr. Marshall, I've got to run to an appointment." The first chapter of *Every Kid A King: The Story of Sacker Catfish Davis* was on the front page.

— - — - —

"Thanks for meeting me," Tucker said.

"Sorry to hear about your suspension," Fisher said, sitting down next to Tucker on a bench at Sam Houston Park. "You doing all right?"

Sunfish swam in the bayou next to a circular concrete drainage runoff, half-submerged with foot-long algae-eater fish attached to the bottom of it. A few hundred feet away, news crews filmed and spectators gawked at the massive eight-foot-long manatee swimming on the surface. The animal had been spotted by park-goers earlier in the day. Several white scars were visible on the manatee's back. Having read very little and written even less on the subject for class, Tucker thought the manatee drifted in the bayou like a white whale.

"I'm suspended, grounded, and I had to accompany my mom to work today across the street at the library," Tucker said. "To make matters worse, I got wait-listed today at the one college I applied to. My classmates who I have been fighting for are choosing their colleges and talking about their summer plans. I might not even graduate high school. All I ever wanted to do was help the little folks, and now I can't even do that."

"What do you mean?"

"I'm suspended indefinitely. The campaign is over. No one is going to listen to a suspended student."

"Did you suspend the campaign?"

"I'm suspended."

"Suspended from what? No one is saying you can't still campaign while suspended from school. What are they going to do, suspend you?"

Tucker shifted his gaze from the bayou to Fisher's eyes. Sure enough, Tucker found the identical stare he had seen in the eyes of the three little folks on his old elementary school's playground who had prayed for the return of a populist. "I'm already suspended," Tucker said, bouncing up from the bench. "Not even the administration crooks could suspend a suspended person."

"You can't suspend this campaign, or quit—it's bigger than you, Tucker," Fisher said. "This is beyond Memorial Independent School District or the Memorial TIRZ. This is the fight for our city. You should read the letters I get every day at my office from other equally misunderstood people who feel inspired by your fight. It is far and away the biggest response I've ever received to a story. You probably saved me from getting fired. I admit that I didn't take you seriously at first. I thought you were crazy, just good for a few entertaining pieces."

"I am crazy," Tucker said.

"I know you are, and I'm a believer," Fisher said. "So are the little folks, the people of Shady Oaks, your classmates, and others like them in Houston you haven't met but who know you already. Even the Governor of Louisiana is talking about your campaign and what it means to people. You got fight, Tucker, and that is rarer than you know. Trust me, I was in Vietnam."

"You were in Vietnam?"

"I was and I had a lot of friends over there just like you. You got that same something. I had it, too, for the first time when I got out of the military. It was like I could do anything when I was back in the world as a civilian. Nothing the world could throw at me could be worse than what I had survived. And the confidence from that knowledge kept me moving forward when things went wrong around me. Things do go wrong, big and small, but that feeling keeps you level when other people get worked up about things that don't really matter. The feeling faded. Like my love for politics. But covering your story these last couple weeks, I almost want to quit my job, challenge Lanny Whiting for mayor, and clean out city hall—and I'm a gay man. Those are long odds, but I believe again that I could make it happen."

"Your odds might be worse than mine—and I'm suspended."

"Right?" Fisher laughed. "I was the senior class president of Jefferson High School also, Tucker. And I was the only kid in my class crazy enough to end up going to fight in Vietnam. More than me though, you have a destiny."

Destiny, Tucker thought. Huey had believed in his destiny, that he was master of his fate, captain of his ship. "I inherited destiny, I reckon, from the Longs."

"The first time I met you, you told me the story of Huey Long getting his high school principal fired after expelling Huey during his senior year."

"The Kingfish wasn't simultaneously running a campaign for school board when he got expelled and he revenged the act," Tucker said. "Still, I bet I could get enough signatures to get Dr. Green fired."

"I'm not saying get your principal fired." Fisher nodded to the water and the news crews. "If a manatee can swim hundreds of miles across an ocean and up in a bayou, then Catfish can at least get back in the water with him."

"Even a suspended Catfish!"

"Especially a suspended Catfish. That's the only way to survive."

Tucker paced in front of Fisher. "When they tried to impeach Huey Long and they had him at his lowest ebb, he came back and defeated the impeachment and then set about licking them all. His supporters flooding the capital, the Kingfish took the attack back to the enemy and became more powerful than he ever was before the impeachment. This is my impeachment hour. They say I don't belong, that I'm a relic, that there are no more populists. That I'm the last."

"What this age needs is a relic to shake it up, an original that doesn't belong to emerge from the wilderness."

"From the swamp."

"Tuck Catfish Davis," Fisher said. "The Last Populist."

Tucker poked Fisher in the chest with his fedora. "I'm going to need an article on the suspension," Tucker said. "And in a favorable light to me."

Fisher held up his hands. "I can't promise anything. I only write—"

"Side by side an article tearing into the administration

and Walker Moore who are conspiring to keep Catfish unjustly suspended."

"I think I'm crossing a dangerous line as a reporter. I can't now be your friend and cover you in politics."

"I thought you were running for mayor."

"Amigo, I'll try my best," Fisher said, getting up to leave.

"We're going to need better than your best, Mr. Hughes," Tucker said. "But given a free week to campaign when I should be at school, being suspended might just be the best thing to ever happen in my educational career." He borrowed a sheet of paper and a pen from Fisher and began to write:

Dear Governor,

It was with great pride that I received your undeserved praise. You telling folks that I strike you as if I were your own son, a political heir to your populism, was the greatest compliment I have received in my time in politics. Sadly, since then I have joined you in our darkest hour, as I was suspended from school for "political campaigning" while hosting my school's talent show. Instead of letting them keep us knocked down and left for dead, I have an idea that might be our rebirth and see us both emerge victorious over our opponents and their undermining ways. I ask you to come down here and support me on the campaign trail during a break in your trial. The greatest governor any state has ever known, and the kid who dared to take on the moneychangers on the bayou!

They moved to impeach Huey Long, threatened and kicked out Earl Long for sticking up for civil rights, and tried to send you to jail and get me to quit. Only history tells us Huey beat the dirty dogs back, Earl defied them on the floor in speech and broke out of the insane asylum they locked him up in, and you and I are still writing our history. We might be the last, but we ain't out of the fight yet. We have a destiny!

Yours,
Tuck Catfish Davis

Tucker walked down to the bayou, to have a look at what the city had never seen in the water.

— - — - —

"Nice tan."

"Finally got out to the polo grounds this weekend," Walker said. "Nothing like a little polo to celebrate the catching of a catfish."

In his office directly below the exterior west clock of Houston's City Hall, Skip Brammer poured two drinks from a stashed bottle of scotch he kept for celebrations. "I knew the little punk would fall flat on his face," Skip said, passing Walker a drink. "To school board."

"To playing hardball," Walker toasted, glowing in his triumph over his suspended adversary. Walker had begun again to believe in the game of life, and that there were rules.

"You and Dr. Marshall showing up really forced the hand of that principal. I don't think she would have done anything otherwise."

"We set our catfish up and caught him hook, line, and sinker."

"More ways than one to clean a catfish."

"What are all those people taking pictures of down there at Sam Houston Park?"

"The manatee."

"The what?"

"Apparently there is a manatee in the Buffalo Bayou. It was spotted on Friday from the Sabine Street Bridge. Of all the places to travel, the thing picked the dirtiest body of water in the country. Nothing but trash and dead bodies in that sewer. How the hell a manatee from Florida ended up in the Buffalo Bayou is anyone's guess. There is a first time for everything."

"A catfish gutted, a silver fox skinned, and a manatee beached in the bayou," Walker said. "I have now seen it all in this town. I should finally be able to enjoy my son's playoff game tonight." He added a splash of water to his scotch and swirled it around. "Synergy was going to hire a campaign manager for me."

"Why?"

"They didn't think I knew how to play hardball," Walker said. He laughed and stared out at the bayou. "I coached this kid—"

"What is it? I'm in the middle of a meeting with Walker here," Skip scolded his assistant, who had stuck his head inside the councilman's office.

"Let me show you," the assistant said. He turned on the television above Skip's head to the local news. A full-haired old man in a white collared shirt Walker knew only as the Silver Fox strummed a guitar and sang into a television camera in front of a log cabin, "Off with King Lanny's head, the phony King of Houston!"

— - — - —

Against the backdrop of a log cabin preserved by the Daughters of the Republic of Texas, Tucker spoke to the crowd Fisher estimated at one thousand. The poor person's hospital, Ben Taub Hospital, towered behind the log cabin. A hundred TUCK DAVIS, EVERY KID A KING yard signs waived in the air, intermingled with the homemade signs like the two next to Fisher, held by middle-aged women in visors and bearing the slogans SUSPEND TAX ZONES, NOT KIDS and SAVE OUR SCHOOLS, RELEASE A CATFISH. The Silver Fox from the school board meeting, guitar strung around his neck, handed Fisher a flier and asked, "Where's Walker Moore?" The crowd was composed of only a few students who had wandered over from the Rice University campus nearby. Presumably the rest were in school and not suspended on a Monday, Fisher hoped.

"Suspend me some more!" Tucker thundered. "We'll march every day. Because I've got some news for the school district and city hall: Stop fiddling around with this city of ours and listen to the people. We will not back down from our destiny. Suspend me, but debate me. Let us march in defiance to the statue of this city's namesake and saddle up his horse. Who rides with Houston?"

Fisher followed on foot, one step behind Tucker, and one step ahead of the news crews that filmed the march live from the Texas Medical Center along the backside of the Houston Zoo and Hermann Park. The march halted traffic on Fannin Street as a thousand people tailed the irregular movements of Tucker's bowlegs, a square dance across the street towards Sam Houston Monument Circle, the marchers singing "This Land is Your Land."

In his newly-altered, bronze double-breasted suit and fedora hat, Tucker ascended the steps of the monument under the statue of Sam Houston on his horse and turned to address the crowd, most of which had been notified of the march by Fisher's article in the paper the day before. Entombed from head to toe in bronze and buttons, his hat in his outstretched hand, a snapshot of Tucker would have passed for a monument. But then Fisher watched the chin dip as the head leaned forward with the curls out front, and the eyes surged to the back of the crowd to pull everyone in closer. Catfish was back in the water.

"When I was just a kid the size of a bronze hoof," Tucker said pointing up to the horse hoof, raised in honor of the wound Sam Houston received in the Battle of San Jacinto, "I collected money at school to help restore this statue. Pennies and the occasional nickel if times were good. I know folks like Mayor Whiting must have scoffed at our efforts, crazy kids saving their pennies to help our old father Sam Houston here. But it was pennies—from little folks—that saved this statue. Not pennies from fat cats who buy and sell our current crop of city leaders like sacks of potatoes in the market place. If y'all elect me to school board, I promise I will end this reign of corruption and make every kid a king. Who's with me?"

A dozen police cars roared down Main Street. The sirens announced to Fisher that the police were probably not with Tucker.

Tucker looked up at the statue of Sam Houston. "Like our city father, let us march to meet our enemies and take back the district!" Tucker called upon the crowd, leading the march east in the direction Sam Houston's finger pointed.

In the opposite direction of the Memorial Independent School District, east towards the San Jacinto Battleground and the victory of Texas Independence over Mexico, Tucker led his troops in reverse of the famous battle and straight into a waiting gaggle of police officers taken by surprise only by the ease of the capture.

— - — - —

Carlos fed the ten different campaign fliers from his backpack into the copy machine and pressed the buttons to make three hundred copies. He was nervous about getting caught in the teachers' lounge without a pass; he did not want to join Tucker on suspension. Carlos did not want to contemplate what penalty using the copier during a class period in the teachers' lounge for political purposes would carry. At his high school on Friday, the entire student body and faculty had to gather in the auditorium and receive a lecture on the prohibition against politics on school grounds, delivered by the head principal. Carlos doubted this was a coincidence after his attendance at the Jefferson High School talent show where he sang "Every Man A King" and watched Tucker get suspended.

Tucker suspended, Carlos fired, and the Silver Fox

banned from Randalson's, it began to weigh on Carlos how many eggs needed to be cracked to make a school board seat omelet. One hundred copies left. Scared he had drawn a passing teacher's attention, Carlos unplugged the noisy copy machine. Nervous, he looked around and held his breath to listen until he was sure he only heard the news on the television screen.

"Holy shit!" Carlos cursed aloud.

The screen showed little kids on the halted Hermann Park children's train watching a handcuffed Tucker shouting for the little folks to not give up the fight.

— - — - —

For Bobby Boudreaux, New Orleans was again rolling in the manner of the Big Easy. From his French Quarter hotel balcony, Bobby had inhaled the morning breeze of fresh coffee and bananas offloaded at the river wharfs tinged with spilled alcohol on the street below. He sensed the tide of the trial turning in his favor for the first time. When an old supporter invited him to be celebrity bartender for a night to take his mind off the trial, Bobby accepted.

Behind the bar of a French Quarter oyster bar, the governor of Louisiana mixed Sazerac cocktails and entertained the growing crowd. Candy danced to a Dr. John song on the jukebox about tripping into the right place at the wrong time.

"It is great to see your smile again, Governor," a customer at the bar said.

"They're going to try to take my smile from me next," Bobby said. "I hope they bury me standing upside down so the federal prosecutor can kiss my smiling ass."

"So I can kiss it too," Candy said.

"Come here, darling," Bobby said to Candy. To the customer at the bar, he said, "When a man gets to be my age, all he wants in life is either a nurse to wipe his ass or a beautiful girl to carry on his arm. I've got both. A man is only as old as the woman he feels."

"I'll drink to that," the customer said.

Bobby held the drink in the air and said to the people in the bar, "To Tuck Davis: if there was ever a person I admired, it is this Ragin' Cajun kid in Texas. The bastards suspend him from school for campaigning, and he turns it back on them and makes them look like the damn fools they are. No kid has ever studied my playbook so astutely. He's a natural, solid gold this Catfish. He's going to do a lot of good for the poor folks of that city. It's good that us Louisianans got us a friend like that in Houston. You want to know how you can help me? Help Tucker Davis. Send money, send your prayers. They're trying to get rough with our kid there, without knowing how tough the little kid is."

A customer at the end of the bar shouted, "Why is it you talk out of both sides of your mouth?"

"So folks like you with half a brain can understand me," Bobby Boudreaux replied. "Who wants another round to pay tribute to Catfish?"

— - — - —

Carlos, Elliott, and Duna sat on the front steps of the jailhouse downtown. Carlos straightened the black bowtie of his valet uniform and replayed the image of Tucker facedown on the hood of the police car warning the children.

"We have to contact his parents," Duna said. "He's in jail."

"I say we wait a few more hours and see what we find out," Elliott said, also in his valet uniform. "For all we know, he's meeting us at Allen's Glen in thirty minutes to go pass out fliers before we valet tonight at Jones Hall."

"You saw him on television handcuffed and screaming," Duna said to Carlos. "He's in jail!"

"We got to bust him out somehow," Carlos said. "We could use money from the campaign fund for a bail bond."

Elliott said, "If we contact his parents, we need to avoid talking to Dr. Davis and try to talk to Mrs. Davis."

"We could try and go through the Silver Fox," Carlos said. "He's old enough to put up bail for Tucker."

"Are you going to the same event I'm going to?" a giant rooster of a man in a tuxedo asked Carlos. Carlos thought the man's mane of red hair was wilder than Tucker's. The man's posture was at an angle, his chest cocked out in front of the entrance to the jail he had emerged from like he was ready to lean into a punch.

"We're just waiting on a friend," Elliott said.

"Is your friend running for school board?"

"Yes," Elliott said.

"Your friend should be right out. He's not being charged with anything either. Nice to have friends in places like this and well-paid lawyers in-house for such legal pickles."

"Are you a friend of Tucker's?" Duna asked.

"We have a mutual enemy," the man said. "When is the school board debate?"

"Wednesday," Duna said.

"This arrest isn't going to help Tucker," Elliott said.

"There's got to be some positive political aspect of being arrested," Carlos said. "We raised more money in three days from Tucker's suspension than during—"

"In what world other than in the windmills of Tucker's mind does getting arrested translate into cash flow?" Elliott asked.

"I've got a plan I think will work," the man interjected. He handed his business card to each of them. "I already took the first step by contacting the Silver Fox—"

"How do you know the Silver Fox?" Elliott interrupted.

"It was once my job to know everyone and every angle," the man said, pulling out an article from the paper.

Carlos looked at the business card and the strange man suspiciously. "What's special about being an oilman?"

"We're battling an oilman," Duna snarled.

"That oilman wasn't *Special Forces*!" the man growled back. Carlos, Elliott, and Duna silently observed the face of the man reddened by the blood that simmered just below the skin.

Carlos read the card again and asked softly, "You were really in the Special Forces, Mr. Kirby?"

"I know I don't look like much to you young bucks," Donovan said, "but before I was an oilman I was a Green Beret, and I went to graduate school at a little place called Vietnam. Is that special enough for you?"

"A Green Beret!" Elliott exclaimed. "I can't believe this."

"I've never seen one except in movies," Carlos mumbled. A Green Beret, Carlos thought, might just help them level the battlefield against the armies backing their opponent.

"Now that I've got your attention," Donovan said, "I will need to get your blessing on my plan tonight. It is going to cost me a fortune, but I think with my resources in this town I can execute it within the small amount of time we've got. The plan is slightly unconventional."

"That's conventional in Tucker's world," Elliott said.

"My plan is not an attempt to usurp you all as the campaign managers either," Donovan said, shaking hands with the Tucker Davis campaign team. "Rather to add another component to the campaign and attack our enemy asymmetrically by waging unconventional warfare."

"You're going to get along great with Tucker," Carlos said. "He wants to dynamite Walker Moore and the moneychangers."

Eight

The strange lack of humidity made it hard for Walker to discern which of the girls jogging wore panties as he drove through Memorial Park. The most pleasant part of Walker's existence was leaving the office slightly early once a week and cutting through the park to follow the joggers to the music of the car radio, windows down on the way to the Polo Club. Walker thought about taking his polo helmet off, since it was scraping against the car roof upholstery, but in less than a mile he would be at the club. He wanted to arrive with it on, in defiance of Tucker's most recent character assassination directed at Walker's love for polo. Tiring of another update on the manatee, Walker switched to the oldies station. Horses neighed loudly on a recorded sound bite of a cowboy's voice halting a cattle drive. The folksy voice of the cowboy, faintly familiar to the ear of Walker, stopped yelling at cattle to solemnly address the radio listeners of Houston:

"Do Houstonians *really* know their school board president? Walker Moore claims his word is as strong as Texas Oak. He also says he had no idea about accepting over fourteen thousand dollars from employees of commercial real estate company Memorial National—over eighty percent of his entire campaign budget last election. Come on Walker, *no* idea? His word sounds more like the strength of scrub oak to me. Do y'all know that on April twenty-third Walker Moore will vote on the Memorial Tax Incremental Reinvestment Zone, proposed by none other than his good friends at Memorial National? That's the company that owns over sixty percent of the land in the zone. Yes, Memorial National will make billions if it passes. Billions of *your* dollars, Houstonians. We made this advertisement so Walker Moore can't claim he had *no* idea. Vote this year for someone whose word is as strong as Texas Oak, vote Tucker Davis. He's the kid y'all call Catfish who knows something about the way us Texans value a man's word. This advertisement was paid for by Veterans For Integrity Over Texas. Veterans For Integrity Over Texas wants to note Walker Moore is not a Vietnam War veteran and had three deferments during Vietnam before landing a safe place in the Texas Air National Guard."

"Tucker Davis isn't a veteran either!" Walker hollered at the trail boss over the radio. The bum steer was Catfish Davis, Walker thought. The hypocrite was using "soft money" for advertisements. How else could his campaign obtain the money to air the first school board election advertisement in the history of radio? Who was this sketchy group, Veterans For Integrity Over Texas? Tucker was suspended and then invited to speak at the Junior League, and, now arrested, was receiving airtime to attack Walker. Walker had worked his whole life to be invited to speak at the Junior League and have his word compared to Texas Oak. Not some scrub oak over the radio. "I know that's your voice, Silver Fox!"

A heavy gust of Cajun seasoning on the wind tickled the trimmed hairs in Walker's nostrils at the central Memorial Park stoplight, directing his attention to a giant red sign that read: TUCKER DAVIS FREED FROM PRISON CAMPAIGN FUNDRAISER AND CRAWFISH BOIL. A long line of homeless people, voters Tucker doubtlessly locked down while sharing a jail cell, snaked around the curve of the running trail for as far as Walker could see.

Walker was done playing in the low ground against this catfish with nine lives. The debate was in four hours. The time had come for political consultants. Turning back around, Walker called the number of the political consultant, informing him of a change of heart. As per his new focused strategy, Walker detoured only to pull up a few Tucker Davis yard signs he felt unfairly taunted him.

Back in his Synergy office, Walker held the black, ten-gallon cowboy hat out between the fingers of both hands as if the mink felt it was crafted out of was a carrier for the plague. "I'm not wearing this."

"You are if you want to win tonight's debate," the political consultant said, holding up the picture of Walker in full polo regalia in the *Chronicle* that Tucker's campaign had planted in the morning edition. "Less polo playing, more goat roping."

"We live in Memorial, the richest area of town."

The political consultant showed a poll from *The Pony Express* with Walker trailing by twelve percent.

"That's Tucker's paper," Walker said. "What legitimate poll has a margin of error of eleven percent?"

"Be grateful you hired me today before this debate and that you're sharing the news with the manatee," the political consultant said, holding up the front-page picture of the manatee.

At the cost of a small fortune, Walker was not grateful. The original plan of the CEO and chief operations officer had now come to pass, but with Walker footing the bill and not Synergy, due to campaign finance laws. Tucker's bump in the polls from his arrest and the sight of his subsequent fundraiser pushed Walker over the edge; Walker would spend whatever it took, pull out all the stops, to defeat Tucker. The political consultant said it was going to cost a lot to pull out all the necessary stops, because with neither adult responsibilities nor school (because of the suspension), Tucker had ample time to prepare for the debate. The political consultant cautioned it was a town-hall style debate, impossible to fully prepare for. A wild card. Walker lowered the black cowboy hat to sit low over his brow, a high-priced recommendation for a less elitist appearance at the debate. Deal me a wild card, Walker thought, slowing his breathing using an acting technique he learned from the University of Houston drama coaches to get into character.

The political consultant and Walker pulled up to the front entrance of the school. Walker unsnapped the top pearl button choking him at his throat. He waddled slowly in his tight blue jeans toward the auditorium entrance feeling more like a rodeo clown approaching a bull than a candidate at a debate.

The auditorium was full. After an introduction by the debate moderator, Dr. Marshall, Walker delivered a brief opening statement urging the voters to perform due diligence on the candidates. Tucker, strangely dressed in the same white dinner jacket Walker had seen him wear as a valet, gave a crazed soliloquy about discovering the little folks and leaving a legacy. Walker felt confident that the audience associated the white dinner jacket with the more appropriate straightjacket Tucker needed to be donning. Questions from the audience followed, most on the Memorial TIRZ. A diverse section of thirty people Walker had never met before, located in the first couple of rows, cheered and screamed, stood and applauded, whenever he spoke. They took their cue from the orchestrating political consultant who sat among them and would dispense their pay after the debate, ultimately from Walker's bank account. Walker watched a lady he had sat next to in church step up to the microphone stand stationed in the left aisle.

"This question is for Mr. Moore. If you were reelected and you remained school board president, what would be your number one priority for next year?"

"Keeping Memorial Independent School District the number one school district in Texas," Walker said. The front row of paid supporters stomped and stood up to clap, starting a wave of cheering that connected with Walker's real supporters. Walker grabbed the brim of his new cowboy hat and tipped it to the cheers. "I would accomplish this by setting the tone that our kids are the top priority. We can raise their test scores even more if we introduce a higher standard to teacher evaluations, just like any other business holding its employees accountable for job performance. Eliminate tenure, I propose. As an executive at Synergy, I have been a part of implementing such an evaluation system, and we have benefited immensely from it. In fact, Synergy has been named the most innovative company for the past five straight years. It is this kind of experience that I bring to the Memorial Independent School District Board of Trustees. My opponent wants to run the district and he is not on the honor roll, was voted class clown, hasn't even been to college, receives donations from indicted Louisiana Governor Bobby Boudreaux and soft money from political action committees, gets suspended, and the only record he's got is a police record. I ask you, who do you want running your school district?"

The crowd lifting him up, Walker tapped into an acting reservoir he did not know he had to add in a drawl, "We don't wear white dinner jackets down here to debates, and we don't find it cool to protest and get arrested in Houston." He attempted to control his breathing to continue yelling in his newfound syntax, "We're just Texans. So let us Texans govern Texas schools. If you want to be a Louisiana populist, go up North to Louisiana with the other Yankees. We still wave old glory in this school district. This here is Texas, y'all! Tell Bobby Boudreaux to keep his dirty money in Louisiana—this is Texas, y'all!" Walker waved the cowboy hat to the hooting crowd. Had there been an American flag, or old glory as he now referred to it, he would have wrapped himself in it onstage. In character, he was out of character, waving the cowboy hat loved by the test audience Walker was paying for.

Tucker shuffled up to the microphone and said, "Attack me all you want President Moore. Make fun of my blue-collar background working alongside some of this city's finest sackers and valets, successfully managing a prom budget and class legacy, organizing the Share Our Wealth Coalition, and picking buckets of blackberries in fields with hands blood-purple." Tucker raised his white palms to the crowd, forgetting it was his mother that picked the bushels of blackberries he ate. "Laugh at all of us without fancy honor roll bumper stickers and golden college diplomas on our walls, but save your hatred of the poor southern folks of our sister state and the great leaders there who tried to give them the whole hog denied to the little folks by corporations like your Memorial National."

Tucker walked up the middle aisle to the third row and addressed both sides of the auditorium, "Corporations that propose a bill stealing your hard-earned money for their own pockets because they don't want to pay taxes like the rest of us. You're lucky, President Moore, a sad country bumpkin like me is your opponent and not the great Huey Long, because he wouldn't abide one minute of the sort of corrupt state our school district is in. Walker Moore is right, I'm guilty. I'm a dyed-in-the-wool Louisiana populist if that means I'm a believer in the little folks and a friend of the working man here in Houston town. If y'all want more of the same, vote Moore. If y'all want every kid a king, a Cajun chicken in every lunch tray with a Dr Pepper for your kids, then vote Tuck Davis. President Walker Moore sure as hell won't be there, but I will be there for you when the levee breaks!"

"First of all, there are no levees in Houston. And I work for Synergy, not Memorial National," Walker said, saving the issue of fried Cajun chicken, soft drinks, and child obesity for another time. "Secondly, there is nothing shady about the tax incremental reinvestment zone. It will give extra money to the school district."

"And to your cronies," Tucker said.

"What cronies would receive extra money? How can you talk? You were arrested this week."

Tucker jabbed his fedora in the air in the direction of Walker. "On the battlefield."

"At a monument paying tribute to the hero of the battlefield," Walker parried, donning his black hat. "The battlefield is in San Jacinto."

"Gentlemen," Dr. Marshall said, reappearing as the moderator from his seat in the front row. "Please return to the front. We will take one last question for tonight's debate."

At the microphone stand in the left aisle was the political consultant, Walker's paid version of the Silver Fox, who lobbed a rehearsed soft-pitch question for waiting cleanup batter Walker Moore, "*Why* are you running for school board?"

— - — - —

"It was a draw," Fisher said.

"The boy wonder didn't slay the dragon?" the editor asked, rocking in his office chair.

"Tucker landed a few shots about the Memorial TIRZ, but Walker defended it as being in the best interest of the school district. The audience appeared to be about half against the Memorial TIRZ, half for it."

"That sounds right because our poll has Walker Moore and Tucker Davis in a dead heat."

Fisher paced back and forth on the other side of the

desk. "Do you think the conflict of interest revelations in my article tomorrow will change the race?"

"The fact that the six-person Memorial TIRZ Board appointed by the city consists of two members of Memorial National, one former city councilman who voted for it, and a partner in Skip Brammer's law firm," the editor said, "is not going to help the cause in the court of public opinion. Brammer's law firm derives a third of its business from representing Memorial National."

"A board with all the powers of a municipality but without the accountability of being elected."

"All the ingredients of a citywide scandal screwing over—"

"The little folks," Fisher said.

"Catfish could not have put it any better," the editor said. "This kid should run for mayor."

The veracity of the statement froze Fisher.

— - — - —

Walker tore off the plastic liner and flipped to the city section of the morning paper in his purple monogrammed robe to read about his debate victory. He was rereading the article MEMORIAL TIRZ BOARD, A CONFLICTED SET OF INTERESTS by Fisher Hughes when his wife came to the front door and screamed at him in the driveway that the political consultant was on the phone.

"Skip didn't tell me any of this. Or that his damn partner was on the board with two Memorial National executives," Walker shouted into the phone, waving the newspaper in the other hand.

"No law prohibits the members of the TIRZ Board of Directors from having a financial interest in the land. It's actually not that abnormal to have a member—"

"You tell Catfish I am the Last Wildcatter for crying out loud, not a cowardly lion."

"No one said anything about you being a cowardly lion," the political consultant said.

"Nor am I some pigeon feeding at the trough of Memorial National as printed here."

"*Pig* feeding at the trough."

"Then I'm whole hog, because there's no conflict of interest with Walker Moore," Walker continued undeterred. "Tucker Davis does not have a monopoly on craziness. I'm not conflicted, I'm crazy."

"Be careful how you let this conflict you. You don't want to anger more people, important people," the political consultant said.

— - — - —

"They're playing dirty with the wrong kid," Tucker said to Donovan, after Donovan swore to Tucker that he had not been followed. They met beside the tracks of the downtown train station. Tucker insisted they cross over the tracks to the abandoned Jefferson Davis Hospital. "They didn't even take my picture when they brought me down to the jailhouse and threw me in a holding cell."

"Couldn't have been cheap to forge this and print it," Donovan said admiring the pamphlet with a mug shot of Tucker on the first page. "I'm not surprised that a man dropped this off with your mother at work today and told her to think about whether she cared about keeping her job."

"He's damn lucky I was reading about Huey Long down in the library basement stacks when he dropped it off," Tucker said. "There's not a true statement in that pamphlet besides the censure I received from a Jefferson High

School ethics panel on falsifying a few signatures for a petition to bring a Dr Pepper machine to school."

"There's a whole lot of money at stake in a tax incremental reinvestment zone. They're not going to let a kid stand in their way."

Tucker smiled at the thought that he stood in the way of Memorial National rolling over the little folks of Houston. "If they want to lie and mix it up," Tucker said, "I can lie and mix it up too on behalf of little folks." Tucker winked at Donovan. "Hell, my pappy thinks I was valeting last night, not debating."

"I'll keep the radio advertisements playing," Donovan said. "The worst thing you can do though is start lying, my friend. This is guerilla warfare because they've got all the money and muscle, but you're winning the battle for the hearts and minds of the people. Now that you're even in the polls with Walker Moore, lying would undercut your campaign's strength as the truth-telling insurgent up against Goliath. I'll keep investigating Walker Moore and Synergy. This isn't my first insurgency."

Tucker picked up a limestone rock. "They can try and punish whoever they want, including my parents, but I'm going to beat them," Tucker said, "and if need be, meet them alone on the battlefield and beat them at their own game of playing dirty. This is bigger than any one person." He threw the rock at a broken hospital window pane. The rock hit and shattered the jagged pane.

"Your mom works for the city as a librarian. Does your father have tenure at Rice?"

"What's tenure?"

"Job security. Something he better have, as I believe Synergy is the largest donor to the university's endowment. I wouldn't be surprised if Memorial National donates millions of dollars as well."

"When I'm finished with these crooked bastards, they

will have wished they stuck to the truth. I think it is about time I ventured forth into the belly of the beast."

"If you start lying and playing by their rules in this fight, you're only walking into the trap they set for you. They are flushing Catfish up to the surface."

"If they want to change the rules," Tucker said, "I will show them I can beat them at their own game."

— - — - —

Dr. Marshall told Dr. Green to rest at ease for a minute after the meeting of school principals concluded at the administration building. Dr. Marshall put his pen down and cracked his knuckles.

"The suspension of Tucker Davis has backfired."

"What do you mean backfired?"

"Backfired in our faces," Dr. Marshall said. "We have this scheming Governor Boudreaux speaking of their shared persecution and creating headlines."

"There is no backfiring, sir," Dr. Green said. "We suspended him because he broke the rule of 'no politics' on school district property."

"He is championed as a hero in the papers, while we look like buffoons for suspending him," Dr. Marshall said. "I don't know about you, but I am not a buffoon."

Dr. Green was unsure regarding the level of her buffoonery. She was certain Dr. Marshall was a buffoon.

"Reinstate him," Dr. Marshall ordered.

"I can't, Tucker was arrested by the police just this week."

"He was detained."

"You sound like him."

"Either way, it was not on school district property," Dr. Marshall said. "He's killing us with bad publicity every day he stays suspended. Reinstate him, and the story dies."

"Must I remind you, sir, there is the principle of the matter," Dr. Green said. "Getting arrested while on suspension is not usually grounds for a student being reinstated."

"Then I will make an executive decision for you," Dr. Marshall said. "He's reinstated."

— - — - —

Dr. Davis tolerated the first two departures with uncharacteristic restraint and pretended not to notice. But the bungled third departure was his favorite student, a mousy little brunette, always overdressed. She tripped on a backpack in an attempt to sneak out quietly through the door when he had his back turned to the class.

"And why are you leaving?" Dr. Davis asked the trapped mouse.

Caught in the act in front of the class she struggled, "I was . . . going to . . . the demonstration."

"*Demonstration*," Dr. Davis repeated for effect. "A demonstration, I take it, that is considerably more important than the role of Fortune in *The Consolation of Philosophy*? Or your grade in this class? Tell us please, what is the quest of this assembly and the people who will assemble there to demonstrate?"

Whispers and stifled laughter erupted from the class. Dr. Davis turned to the class and asked, "Am I the only one in this classroom who doesn't know about this demonstration?"

"It is . . . a rally . . . for," the girl said, unable to say it.

"Catfish Davis," a student in the class disliked by Dr. Davis shouted out.

"He's here? *My* son?"

"He's in the main quad," the girl said.

"But he's grounded," Dr. Davis said.

Dr. Davis thundered past the girl. He left his briefcase on the front desk. Cutting through the lawns of spacious oak trees on the Rice University campus, he barreled under the Moorish arches surrounding the main campus quad where hundreds of students surrounded a bronze-suited speaker who stood atop a golf cart used by campus security.

"I came up here to get the kids involved because they say y'all don't get involved in politics," Tucker said through a bullhorn to the crowd. Unable to walk about on the small golf cart roof, Tucker stood still, though Dr. Davis did not mistake his son from afar for a statue of the school founder. "We might be from different generations, you and me, but we're of the same mind when it comes to battling corruption. A trusted informant of mine showed me evidence earlier today that this lying buzzard mayor and city council of ours are planning to make the next tax incremental reinvestment zone here at Rice, taking away some of this land that is yours. Let them try. I'll take you Rice Owls any day over them buzzards in a fight. I don't care what the odds are or the size of their horde or how much money they pump into the university endowment to try and sway the university board in their favor! Take your TIRZ and take your tenure!"

A ragtag mob of the Rice student band in wrinkled blue suits and gray fedora hats blew horns at random and yelled, "Charge!" The students—some of Dr. Davis' students—were cheering the speaker. Dr. Davis put his head down as they cheered. The populist began to talk the parliament of owls out of their tree.

"I need your support, and I need it now, be it money, putting out campaign signs, passing out fliers, demonstrating tomorrow at the school board vote on the TIRZ, or anything y'all can do to see we take it to these buzzards and get elected next week. I came out here today to say owls and catfish got a stake in this together."

Tucker descended the golf cart roof with the help of an old man. Dr. Davis wondered if the old man was the Silver Fox from the paper. Dr. Davis pushed forward in the crowd in order to halt the madness that had now invaded the sanctuary of higher learning. The golf cart had stopped near the front of the school.

"Can we ask you a few questions for the school paper?" a reporter from the Rice student paper asked Tucker.

"Only a few. We have to get the candidate somewhere else," Elliott said.

"Hell, y'all can ask whatever y'all want. This ain't the Walker Moore campaign."

"Do you think of yourself as a green candidate?" the reporter asked.

"I'm like the manatee, I'll roll around in brown water if I have to. My fight is for the little folks, making sure they get what's theirs."

"You believe indicted Governor Bobby Boudreaux is a good governor?"

"I know he's a great governor, and a good friend of mine and little folks everywhere. One of the greatest governors this country has ever seen."

"Would you vote for a gay member of school board?"

Elliott held up a clipboard in front of the reporter. "That's enough questions."

"I would if the person were the best person for the job," Tucker said. "I got one good friend who is gay. I don't know much about gays, but if he's full of fight and a friend of the people, then he's my man for the position."

"So you are against discrimination like the 'Don't ask, don't tell' policy on gays?"

"That has nothing to do with the school board election," Elliott protested.

"Catfish stands against all discrimination of humans," Tucker said. "I don't know this policy, but I do know that gay folks, like all little folks, got rights too. That's why you can't let them build a TIRZ here at Rice."

"On what information are you basing the statement

that the City of Houston is even considering designating the university area as a TIRZ?" the reporter asked.

Tucker put his fedora on. "Don't believe them when they lie to you and say otherwise, because y'all will wake up the next morning to high rises looking down at y'all."

Elliott turned and dropped his clipboard at Dr. Davis' feet. "Dr. Davis, what are you doing here?"

"I teach here," Dr. Davis said. "What the hell are you two doing?"

"Dealing with the press, Dad," Tucker said, shaking the hand of the reporter. "We were campaigning here, making a push to get some owls aboard this campaign for the final leg. Silver Fox, have you met my old man?"

"Are you trying to get me fired, Tucker?" Dr. Davis asked.

"What do you think about your son campaigning for school board at Rice, Dr. Davis?" the reporter asked Dr. Davis, who limply shook hands with the Silver Fox. Dr. Davis recognized the reporter as another one of his more irksome students.

"I think he's grounded," Dr. Davis said, raising his hand to cut off any more questions.

"*Was*," Tucker said high-fiving the open palm of his father's hand. "Got reinstated earlier just in time to rally and continue the fight over the school board vote on the Memorial TIRZ. Crazy, huh?"

Nine

In his first act upon being reinstated to school, Tucker kicked everyone out of *The Pony Express* office.

"When the newspapers controlled by the old guard and big business kept running Huey Long down and wouldn't play fair, he started his own paper with political cartoons and editorials attacking the other lying candidates and papers," Tucker said to Duna. He passed her a piece of paper with short editorials and a poorly drawn cartoon of a catfish boxing the many tentacles of a giant squid. "My idea is a one page supplement inside *The Pony Express* that stands alone as a paper for this campaign called *The Pelican*."

"You receive great press though, Tucker," Duna said. "*The Pony Express* has printed profiles, editorials, chapters of your autobiography, and this week we even bumped an article on Chuck Moore's baseball scholarship to the University of Texas for another one on you."

The classroom door opened and Elliott ducked through it carrying a bag of popcorn. "I thought I might find you in here," Elliott said to Tucker. "Where is everyone?"

"The election is on Monday," Tucker said to Duna. "All I would need is a special printing of the paper on Election Day to distribute to voters in aiding their voting and telling the whole story. It doesn't have to be called *The Pelican,* but I figured it was a solid name for it since the pelican is the state bird of Louisiana."

"I'm going to have to tell you we can't do it."

"You're my prom date, but you won't publish *The Pelican*?"

"Is that why I'm your date, Tucker? Did you ask me to prom when you announced for school board because you wanted me to cover you in the paper? I think that was the first time that you had spoken to me since I transferred here two years ago. Now you come in here in the mornings and tell the rest of the staff to leave the office."

"Why does that not surprise me?" Elliott cried.

"I kicked them all out so we could hash out a deal," Tucker said. "I didn't want to propose the idea of *The Pelican* in front of them and leave them with the idea I was strong-arming a deal out of you."

"Isn't that exactly what you are doing?" Duna asked.

"Yes," Tucker said, "that's why I kicked them out."

"Don't you see how unethical all this is? I'm the editor, not you."

Tucker showed her the pamphlet with the doctored mug shot on the first page. "Are these lies ethical? We're on the same team, Duna. You're the architect of the Tuck Davis campaign. You came up with the TIRZ idea, you kept the campaign in the press when I got suspended, and you were there to help bail me out when I got arrested."

"I didn't report on the Memorial TIRZ to help your campaign create a political wedge. It's a real issue facing people. I'm on your team, but not like this." Duna dropped her head in her hands. "I can't keep doing this, Tuck. I've got to focus on the future."

"This is the future. Tonight they vote on the TIRZ. Next week the election."

"I'm dropping out of the campaign."

"You can't drop out of the campaign. You are the campaign!"

"I can't go to prom with you either," Duna said. "I'm sorry."

"I'll tell you why you have to go," Tucker said, trying to negotiate with Duna who pushed past him, crying. Tucker ran to the door and yelled down the hall at her, "I've been campaigning for you for prom queen!"

"What are you doing?" Elliott asked Tucker in the hallway.

"Should I have allowed Duna to kick the staff out, instead of me kicking them out? I'm not wedded to *The Pelican* as a name. Duna can name the supplement after the Texas state bird."

"I've told you that your Kingfish tactics and beliefs do not translate with Duna," Elliott said. "You just scared away the one girl that might ever allow you to get to first base. If *you* don't care about winning Duna over, why the hell have I been killing myself campaigning for you? Dammit Tuck, in a half year we'll be in the twenty-first century and those bowling shoes you're wearing won't be so cool." Elliott shook his head and handed Tucker the bag of popcorn.

Alone in the hallway, Tucker looked down at his black and white two-toned shoes that went so well with his cream-colored, double-breasted suit. Strangely, the new polish had not seemed to impress Duna. Confused by losing Duna's vote, Tucker redoubled his efforts, cornering a dozen students in the hall about the school board vote, his bowlegs like a vise preventing escape, before running into Mrs. Bridge.

"Welcome back, Tucker," Mrs. Bridge said. "I just read the fourth chapter of your sacking memoir and a corrected copy is on my desk."

"May I talk to you for a second?"

Mrs. Bridge directed him to her classroom. "Are you concerned about your grade?"

Tucker sat down at his desk and thought for a second if his failing grade was a concern. "I'm concerned about the union endorsement. I need some good news, Mrs. Bridge."

"I have an answer for you, though I need to explain a few things. We voted the day after the debate. In a close vote, the union decided to endorse you, but because you are the only alternative to Walker Moore and his proposal to scrap tenure for teachers."

"I'll take it. No need to second guess, y'all have made the right decision," Tucker said. "It came down to the question of tenure, huh?"

"Yes," Mrs. Bridge said, "and one caveat, Tucker. The union was very uneasy about your run-ins with controversies. If you should be arrested again, for example, we will withdraw our endorsement and endorse no one. The teachers wanted me to make clear to you and the press that we are not really for you, as much as we are one hundred percent against Walker Moore's plan to do away with tenure and offer incentive-based pay."

"That was his only original idea."

"You're for it?"

Tucker smiled. "I just got my first union endorsement. I'd be a damn fool to create controversy the first day. However, I want to warn you and the union that something might come out in the papers about me telling a crowd at Rice about taking away tenure. I just want to clarify that comment was in regards to cutting teaching tenure only at the university level."

— - — - —

The Churchill Room at the Black Labrador Pub was for private parties. A history buff, Walker loved the room's musty shelves full of volumes on and by Winston Churchill and walls covered in portraits and pictures of the great twentieth-century leader. Wooden beams from the galley of an old tall ship ran across the ceiling of the room centered on a fireplace. Walker found Skip at a table full of Memorial National executives.

"President," Skip said.

"Hello, lads, I should've known I'd find you all here plotting together," Walker said. "I should have brought along my old classmate and friend Fisher Hughes to document this. What a follow-up story this would make for the paper."

"You're reading the wrong paper."

"I thought I was too, *old* friend. I thought, Fisher Hughes must have his facts wrong, he doesn't know the entire story. But I did some research of my own and talked with some of your colleagues at city hall, and apparently Fisher knows you better than I do, Skip."

"You're reading the wrong paper, Walker. Read this one," Skip said, holding up the Rice University paper. "Tucker endorsed gay candidates. We've finally got him set up for the kill." In the other hand, he lifted up the pamphlet with Tucker's mug shot on the first page. "Combined with a second printing of these to be shipped out tomorrow."

"Did you not think I would eventually find out that you are in bed with these guys, Skip?" Walker asked, flicking his hand towards the Memorial National executives at the table. "Have you forgotten your own speech about doing the right thing for the future of Houston? Did you think you were conning me again into pushing a cow up to the top of the stairs?"

"It's still what is best for the city. You *want* conflicts of interest in a TIRZ."

A portrait of Churchill among the bombed ruins of the Battle of Britain hung over the fireplace behind Skip's head, the proximity a sacrilegious offense to Walker, who had read hundreds of history books on the era and identified that the two men had nothing in common. No historical figure had failed and picked himself back up from failure more than Churchill. Holding vigil at rock bottom, Churchill rose again by blood, toil, tears, and sweat to lead alone a nation and world in their most perilous test. Tucker could have Huey P. Long and his crazy brother Earl; Walker, the Last Wildcatter, would take Winston S. Churchill, the Last Lion.

Fifty-three-year-old Walker B. Moore looked above Skip to Churchill and spoke to ears beyond the Churchill Room, "We shall neither flag nor fail in our solemn duty to serve our school district best. We shall fight greed and the corrupt people who feed off of it in the bayous and on our interstates. We shall never, never, never, never, never surrender to Memorial National Incorporated or its like, and as long as the people remark on this campaign and pitched battle against the TIRZ, they will still say, 'This was our city's finest hour.'"

"What oath is that?" Skip asked. "This vote is once in a lifetime."

"You do your worst, and we shall do our best!" Walker said. His hand formed a raised V-victory sign in the silent room, the former cowardly lion, defiant, in the lion's den, under the unflinching stare of the Last Lion.

— - — - —

Dr. Green was dialing the office of Dr. Marshall when the second and third news stations showed up. "Channels eleven and thirteen news crews are here now and want permission to interview Tucker Davis also," Mrs. Bryce said to Dr. Green.

"Tell them to wait in the lobby until after I get off the phone," Dr. Green said.

"This is Dr. Marshall."

"This is Dr. Green. We have a bit of a situation here. Three news stations have arrived in the last fifteen minutes wanting to interview Tucker Davis about the school board race. I know there can be no politics on school district property, but I wanted to call and let you know they showed up. Do you want me to say anything to them specifically when I go talk to them?"

"Thank you for notifying me. I have no problem with them interviewing the student about the race. Pass on that I will be too busy to make any comments on air about it today."

"Dr. Marshall, I thought we weren't going to allow anything related to politics on school district property. I suspended Tucker Davis for a week after he violated the rule you imposed."

"This is a case-by-case basis sort of thing, Dr. Green. Please inquire whether the interview segments will be running live or on one of the later newscasts."

Case-by-case. Dr. Green wondered what case this was as she hung up the phone. "Mrs. Bryce, send for Tucker Davis," Dr. Green said, stepping out of her office. A tall, black-haired woman in a business suit collided with Dr. Green.

"Are you Dr. Green?" the woman asked.

"Who are you?"

"I'm Diane Lieker with Channel Eleven News. I was going to see if we could interview school board candidate Tucker Davis for the news tonight."

"Are all of you here because of the vote tonight on the Memorial TIRZ?"

"That and I had some questions for him about an interview he did with a college paper and some of his comments."

"What were his comments regarding? I'm not acquainted with the article."

"About gays."

"Gays?"

"Gay rights. Here look at this."

"SCHOOL BOARD CANDIDATE FIGHTS FOR GAY

RIGHTS," Dr. Green read the Rice University paper front-page headline aloud.

— - — - —

Tucker's hands clasped, grabbed, shook, and pulled everyone entering the Memorial Independent School District administration building; the bowlegs rounded up any loose strays from the herd. Tucker wanted all ears.

"How's it look in there?" Tucker asked.

"Been standing room only for the last twenty minutes," Carlos said. "Every person in there is holding one of our fliers. The Silver Fox is leading them in chants. I was thinking the cheering might only harden the resolve of stubborn school board members, though. I think you should talk to the Silver Fox and have him holster the cheering."

Tucker laughed at the simple-mindedness of this suggestion from his loyal campaign manager. "Don't I pay you to run my campaign and for political advice? A show of force is the only thing these brutes will understand—you know that. Like the rally at Sam Houston Monument Circle, I went directly to the people and captured victory through surprise attack."

"I wasn't able to attend because *I* wasn't suspended, but as I recall, you were arrested."

"Speaking of technicalities, is there a Citizens Participation portion in the meeting tonight?"

"No," Carlos said.

"Has Duna shown up yet?"

"No."

"Can you try calling her again? I want her to be a part of this tonight, win or lose."

"Sure, but Elliott doesn't think she's going to come."

"I wrote a speech for tonight, and I was going to have her look at it."

"You never stick to your written speeches or the topics Duna gives you."

"I was going to try to tonight," Tucker said. He passed Carlos the speech. Handwritten in blue ink on the last page was a reminder to thank friends Huey Long, Earl Long, Bobby Boudreaux, and staff Duna, Elliott, and Carlos.

"Vote no TIRZ!" rattled off the walls as Tucker and Carlos journeyed toward the overflowing room.

"Vote no TIRZ!" Tucker chanted as he pushed his way to the front where the Silver Fox waved his hands.

"Vote no TIRZ!" the Silver Fox led the chanting crowd. Tucker popped through the crowd and joined the Silver Fox. "They're all yours," the Silver Fox said to Tucker.

Tucker held out his arms like a martyr on a cross, his crown of thorns a tan fedora. He waited on the crowd, knowing they had waited too. Carlos bowed and presented Tucker's rolled-up speech. Tucker thanked him with a smile. Tucker saw the superintendent and all seven school board members were at their seats with their eyes on him.

"It's not like me to stay on script and read y'all one of these," Tucker said. He raised the speech above his head so the crowd in the back could see. "But I'm going to try in the couple of minutes we've got until this kicks off." Tucker looked and saw no movement by Walker to commence with the start of the meeting; he waited on Tucker.

Dr. Marshall said into his microphone, "This meeting cannot and will not start, son, until you are seated and—"

"Vote no TIRZ!" the Silver Fox yelled.

"They want us to be quiet so they can hurry this meeting and vote in their tax zone. I would have thought these last three weeks would have shed some light on this issue," Tucker bellowed. "That we don't want our taxes going into the pockets of swine, fat cats, and buzzards."

Tucker unrolled his speech and read aloud to the audience, "Y'all came here tonight to show little folks have a say in their government, too, and the way things are run. The members of the Board might forget who elected them to office as they count up their gold, but next week when y'all have to vote to re-elect them, y'all will remember the way they vote tonight."

Tucker thrust his fedora in the direction above the school board members' heads and said, "Give every kid one of these crowns when y'all vote tonight against passing this special tax zone for the rich, and make every kid a king, no matter how you once promised you would vote. I'm reminded of what an administrative aide was once told by Uncle Earl, who, along with his brother Huey Long, Governor Boudreaux, and my staff of Elliott Taylor, Duna Shari, and Carlos Ortega, I would like to personally thank for helping me in this fight for school board."

"No one cares what Earl Long said," Dr. Marshall said. "Sit down and be quiet so we may start."

The crowd booed Dr. Marshall and cheered, "Let Tucker speak!"

Dr. Marshall relented. "What did your Uncle Earl say so we can carry on?"

"What our old Uncle Earl told his administrative aide to say to an angry mob of fat cats demanding to see Earl, who had promised them a construction bill—Earl freely pocketing their money and later reneging on his promise when the legislature convened," Tucker said, pointing his fedora at the school board members, "'Tell them I *lied*!'" Tucker pushed his hat further back on his head and walked over to the side wall.

"This being a meeting of the Memorial Independent School District Board of Trustees to vote on the proposed Memorial TIRZ, and not a regular meeting, there will be no Citizens Participation portion of the meeting," Walker said, "or anything else considered beyond a straight up and down vote by the board of trustees on the proposal. As rules dictate, we will start in numerical order of the seats and finish with the president."

"Not in favor," seat number one school board member said. The room cheered and waited.

"Not in favor," seat number two school board member said.

"In favor," seat number three school board member said. Boos, hisses, and shouts flew through the room.

"In favor," seat number four school board member said.

Tucker began to wonder if they had understood what Uncle Earl had said.

"Not in favor," seat number six school board member said.

"In favor," seat number seven school board member said.

Seat number five school board member and president Walker Moore paused to look at Tucker. Tucker mouthed, "*Tell them I lied.*" Walker said into the microphone, "Not in favor."

— - — - —

"Walker Moore voted against it?" the editor asked. He stopped filling up his coffee in the *Chronicle* break room.

"I couldn't believe it," Fisher said. "The bill was defeated by his vote, four to three. Memorial National must want to kill Walker Moore. They lost out on billions of dollars."

"All because of a school board."

"All because of a catfish!"

"Here he is," the editor said. He turned up the local news on the television. "Look at that outfit. How is this kid winning in those suits?"

On screen, Fisher saw the interview was a taped piece as Tucker spoke outside the auditorium in the sunlight.

"But that is what you said?" a female reporter asked Tucker.

"Hell, I don't know if I agree with myself half the time. I've been talking nonstop to reporters and speaking at rallies most days during this campaign. Tucker Davis fights for a lot of things, and that's why they call me Catfish. The Tucker Davis Campaign is focused on defeating the tax incremental reinvestment zone and winning next week."

"The university paper says you would vote for a gay member of school board and you are quoted as saying, 'I got one good friend who is gay. If he's full of fight and a friend of the people, then he's my man for the position.' Are you now saying you didn't say that? That you wouldn't fight for gay rights?"

"*I'm* the gay friend, chief," Fisher said.

Tucker momentarily walked off camera and then came back straight at the camera. "I'm a friend of the little folks," Tucker said. "A populist. I don't know what that means to you, the next guy, or to my lying enemies, but it means Huey Long and Earl Long and Bobby Boudreaux to me. And Catfish Davis even. If these gays ain't got anyone fighting for them, and it sure sounds like they are little folks, then hell, count me in. I'd be proud to fight for them and get them a fair shake just like I'm trying to do for the folks of the Memorial Independent School District. Folks got rights, and it's a right to not have to wait for your rights and get trampled on."

Onscreen, the news transitioned to a special investigative report on how to break out of a sinking car driven into the bayou.

"Add gay rights activist to his résumé," the editor said, "and loser of the 'School Board Race of the Century.'"

— - — - —

"How did you know to find me here on a Saturday?" Walker asked Donovan. Walker's real question was how Donovan, who seated himself across from Walker's desk, passed through the Synergy front desk security. Walker read the sewn-on coat of arms pocket patch on the forest green blazer Donovan wore: SPECIAL FORCES ASSOCIATION. Donovan Kirby, who at their last meeting told Walker and the rest of the people dining, "Mess with the best, die like the rest," flashed his teeth at Walker and, on his finger, twirled the black mink felt cowboy hat that had been atop the chair he was sitting in.

"I have information you're not going to enjoy hearing."

"You're behind the Veterans For Integrity Over Texas advertisements."

"That is true, however, not the bad news I was going to talk with you about."

"That one of my best friends since childhood was manipulating me for money? Or that you've come to rain down death on me because I'm solely responsible for screwing you and your company? Take a ticket and get in line. I think I am the most hated man in this city."

Donovan sniffed the brim of the hat. "Do you know of a company named Energy Education?"

"It's an energy consulting firm that has a contract proposal being considered by the Memorial Independent School District," Walker said. "It's public record."

"I'll tell you what isn't public record," Donovan said. "Dr. Marshall is a paid consultant for the company. Did you know that?"

Walker let his forehead fall and bang the desk. "Why don't you just tell me that I have no friends. That son of a bitch brought the proposal to the school board," Walker said, talking to the floor, keeping his clean nape down and exposed for the executioner. "He never disclosed he was a paid consultant for the company. Are you sure?"

"That's not all. Energy Education was recently acquired by Synergy for five hundred million dollars. Before that it was a limited partnership run concurrently by the person who was, and is, Synergy's chief financial officer. Energy Education's plan also recommends fixed-rate energy contracts with, guess who?"

Walker shot up and said, "Don't be ridiculous, Donovan, the chief financial officer of one company can't run another business and then sell it to the same company. Our board of directors would never sign off on such a conflict-of-interest. Plus, I work for Synergy, wouldn't I know if we owned this consulting firm?"

"I would look into it for the sake of your own ass, Walker. These bullshit byzantine accounting practices and convoluted subsidiary structures look like the tip of the fucking iceberg," Donovan said, standing up to leave. He set the cowboy hat on Walker's desk. "I don't care what school they went to or how much they are showered around town, I know your top two aren't worth a shit integrity-wise. They can have all the ratings and rankings and the rush of being the coolest at the game, because I know they wouldn't have a set of nuts between the two of them if they were put in a tight spot. It turns out I might owe you for screwing me over."

Walker dialed Dr. Marshall's office at the administration building. No answer. Walker dialed Dr. Marshall's home phone. No answer. Walker wanted an answer on Energy Education. Walker thought of Donovan Kirby as a trusted man whose word was solid—not unlike Texas Oak. Walker packed up his briefcase. He would go visit Dr. Marshall. Walker would get to the bottom of this mysterious Synergy subsidiary, Energy Education. Then he would pay a call to the CEO and chief operations officer.

Passing by the war room on his way out, Walker ran into the chief operations officer critiquing the CEO's stroke with his pitching wedge. They were dressed in full golfing attire as if they had come to play a round in the Synergy building.

"What the hell were you thinking last night?" the chief operations officer barked at Walker.

"Why did you back out last night, Walker?" The CEO sliced the air with his golf club at full speed. "Do you know what this does to your reputation and the reputation of this company?"

Walker practiced his baseball swing in the air. "I was playing hardball."

"*Hardball*? We leaked that gay rights story so you could still vote for the TIRZ and win the race. Answer for your absurd behavior."

"As absurd as a company quietly acquiring a business owned by its own chief financial officer without disclosing the connection? Or absurd like having, oh I don't know, Synergy donate an auditorium so it can secure long-term, fixed-rate energy contracts with the district whose superintendent it quietly employs?"

"We thought you knew about Energy Education." The CEO handed the golf club to the chief operations officer. "There are always conflicts of interest in any good business opportunity. You know this, Walker—you're a president."

"I know," Walker said, "president of the school board."

"Don't act innocent, Walker," the chief operations officer said, twirling the club in the air. "The auditorium has your fucking name on it. We don't donate multimillion dollar auditoriums out of kindness."

"I dressed up in a lion costume and played a cowardly lion for this company, onstage, before my wife."

The chief operations officer smashed the golf club into the conference room table. "You need to pull your head out of your lion's ass and ask for a revote as president. You cost this company hundreds of millions of dollars when we're at a crucial juncture with our stock price."

"Demand a revote," the CEO said, taking the bent golf

club from the chief operations officer and passing it to Walker. "You have always been a team player."

"First as a white knight and then when we needed to play hardball, I know," Walker said. The Last Wildcatter searched for an appropriate historical quote and instead resorted to the last Winston Churchill line in the biography he had been reading before he fell asleep: "There will be *no* peace with Germany." Failing to understand the Churchill allusion fully himself, Walker swung the golf club like a baseball bat into the Synergy logo on the conference room wall.

— - — - —

Two days to go, thought Dr. Green, as she searched the school parking lot for news vans through the blinds in her office. No vans. No reporters. No story. An empty parking lot.

A media tornado had once followed Dr. Green for a week. The story of the graduation condom and the principal had even made brief national news. The low point in her career in education, Dr. Green had rashly stopped graduation ceremonies when a disrespectful student handed her a condom in exchange for his diploma. Her apology, later, meant little to the students who did not get to walk across the stage. Dr. Green survived calls for her resignation and was now the second longest serving principal in the district. Stay in the eye of this storm and let it pass like all the others, Dr. Green knew. Why, then, had Dr. Marshall let the camera crews interview Tucker yesterday and throw a crate of explosives into the fire? *No politics*. It was all politics. Gay rights was not just unchartered territory on the map used by a public high school principal. It was a blank space in Texas where ships fell off at the end of the world. A place only Tucker dared to travel.

There was a soft knock at her door. "Come in," Dr. Green said.

The crooked smile cut across the face of the man in the green blazer in an apology acknowledging the mischievousness landing him in the principal's office. To Dr. Green, he looked like a man who, as a boy, was not unfamiliar with the principal's office and who often tried to smile his way out of an offense. Complimenting his crooked smile, his nose began in one direction before finishing in another. Reddish hair askew, he was not altogether unattractive, possessing what Dr. Green thought of as unconventional good looks. To her utter surprise, Dr. Green found herself hoping the stranger brought news of Tucker.

"Excuse me, Dr. Green, for bothering you on a Saturday," the man said, "but Tucker Davis informed me you don't yet have a date to prom tonight."

— - — - —

"Tucker!" Duna exclaimed as she opened the front door of her family's apartment. Behind Tucker, Elliott cradled a bouquet of yellow roses.

Tucked placed his fedora over his heart. "May we come in?"

"Why aren't you on your way to prom?"

"I can't go to prom without my prom date and campaign public relations chief."

"I told you I can't go to prom with you."

"At the time I hadn't given you the formal position of public relations chief, had I?" Tucker patted down his wet hair which almost immediately sprang back up. "I came by to tell you that you don't have to be on my campaign staff or run another article or publish *The Pelican* supplement. I only want to take you to our senior prom, Duna. I reckon I was wrong to mix our friendship and politics, but politics is what I'm used to and comfortable dealing with. I don't know how to talk about anything else, but I'd like to try.

Hell, I'm still willing to bet if you come with me I can make sure a prom queen's crown sits atop your beautiful head by the end of the night."

"He's not kidding, Duna," Elliott said handing her the yellow roses. "He's been pushing hard for it, with no thought to ethics, or ethnics, as you know."

"This is too easy to rig," Tucker whispered romantically, getting down on one knee. "I'm the one counting the votes."

"I wish I could. I followed the news of your victory and the Memorial TIRZ defeat at the school board meeting. My parents cannot believe you did it."

"It was you who did it, Duna," Tucker said, rising back up to shake her hand. "You were the one who raised the issue of the Memorial TIRZ in the first place and lit the fuse for the dynamite. Accept my apology and let me pay you back by showing you a grand time on the town tonight." Tucker stopped shaking her hand and held it with both of his hands. "No politics. You have my word. And a prom queen tiara."

"I can't, Tucker. I don't have a dress."

"I thought you might say that." Tucker snapped his fingers twice, sending Elliott to his truck. "I, for one, understand. You've been too busy campaigning."

"We couldn't afford to—"

"I never paid you your salary," Tucker continued. "Luckily, we have had an influx of funds this week ahead of Election Day from Donovan Kirby to cover some back expenses."

"You did not!" Duna said as Elliott presented a black sequin dress on a hanger.

"I advised against it as well," Elliott said. "We have to account for all the funds, and the flowers and a formal black dress could be a huge black eye."

"All of them city hall piss-ants steal too—I'm just

honest enough to give some back! It should fit decently, Duna, as I talked with your mom about what size to get and had your dad tailor it. All right, we've got an hour until prom starts and we still have thirty-two campaign signs in the back of Elliott's truck to put in the ground around town."

"It's a beautiful dress, Tucker," Duna said, starting to cry.

"It's got more scales than an alligator gar and fit for a prom queen. I also figured you might need it at some *Chronicle* dress functions this summer for the internship I arranged for Fisher Hughes to get you. Does this mean you're in?"

"Yes!"

"There's no need to cry," Tucker consoled. "I already checked with my source, and you're registered to vote. That's great, because we're going to need everything you got these last couple days as they're trying to tar and feather me on this gay issue. Tonight, dance. Tomorrow, politick."

"Tucker, you have a phone call," Mrs. Shari said, handing Tucker the phone.

"Catfish speaking," Tucker said into the phone.

"Catfish," said a voice Tucker recognized instantly, "your governor is coming to town."

— - — - —

Fisher looked at his watch. He had been covering Walker's first campaign appearance on the Spring Branch side of town for three hours. Walker attempted to give a campaign bumper sticker to a man behind a dry-cleaning counter.

"Is this your store?" Walker asked. The man did not move. "I'm a businessman myself. Can I give you one of these? You can put it on your car or here in your store window."

The man laughed. Walker looked confused. Fisher recognized the cultural exchange, walked over and explained to the man in Vietnamese that his friend was a politician and that his friend wanted to give him a campaign sticker for the store.

"*Khong sao.*"

"He says, 'No problem.'" Fisher bowed slightly and thanked the man, "*Cam on.*"

"One doesn't usually have to bow in Vietnamese culture unless it is a formal setting," Fisher explained to Walker outside as they walked down the shopping strip. "When I was there, it was foreign for the Vietnamese to shake hands. That was one thing we introduced that sort of caught on there."

"You still speak fluent Vietnamese?"

"Fluently on a playground of first graders attuned to John Wayne war movies, yes."

"How did you know he was Vietnamese?"

"For one, his name is Nguyen, the most common Vietnamese name. And if you haven't noticed, every other sign on this street is in Vietnamese."

"I knew one of the areas over here was heavily Korean. You might have won me a vote."

"Anytime," Fisher said. "I know Tucker canvassed this block a week ago so the people here shouldn't all be unaware of the election on Monday."

"I wish I'd gone to Vietnam." Walker stopped and faced Fisher. "Looking back, that is my biggest regret. The one thing I feel I missed out on. When you're young, Vietnam is just a distraction." Walker's gaze drifted back to the dry cleaner's window covered in Vietnamese writing. "It would have made me a better businessman too, you know? Look at Donovan Kirby at Sundance Oil & Gas."

"Donovan's camp was less than ten clicks from where I was during most of my second rotation in Vietnam." Fisher bent over to tie the flopping rubbery shoe strings of his topsiders. "You didn't miss out on anything. Except a lot of sitting around with your thumb up your ass and the occasional incident that, with enough embellishment, could be turned into a war story back in the states if told with the requisite affected thousand-yard stare. You've got to have that stare when you tell war stories. That stare is the key to a successful telling. Without that stare, how can they believe you've seen the horror? The horror."

"I mean it, though. I feel like you experienced something key to life the rest of our generation missed out on. A member of a real fraternity, not the stupid one I was president of in college. There's always a divide between veterans and non-veterans, even the way you all converse when you're around each other."

"It was the high-water mark of my life, Walker, and I can't remember a damn thing worth repeating or any lessons I took out of it. If anything, I learned not to take myself too seriously because no one cares. I cringe when I hear business executives with military experience talk about how the military taught them how to lead and manage people and communicate. For the love of God, those self-congratulating idiots knew how to do all of that before the war just like all humans do. That's just something to hold over everyone's head who didn't serve. I do it all the time myself now that I think about it—it's a great card to play. Though my biggest regret is the number of times I've played it."

Walker in the lead, they stumbled into a restaurant that Walker had thought from the outside was a fish store. Fisher recommended they bury the ghost of Vietnam over some Vietnamese seafood. He thought life too depressing to refight wartime decisions they had made thirty years before.

"What brought on your eleventh-hour switch on the Memorial TIRZ?" Fisher asked, after ordering them both several dishes of steamed fish and grilled shrimp in Vietnamese.

"I know I'm not really the Last Wildcatter as you call me, but I am the president of the school board. The craziest thing is, it took Tucker Davis for me to realize it—and that I could save the district and the city from a disastrous mistake. I might be out of a job, and soon out of public office, but I made my stand."

"You're out of a job?"

"I think we can assume I am, as I was ordered to hold a school board revote on the Memorial TIRZ and I'm not going to do it. I also left the office today after playing baseball with the Synergy logo in our conference room. And for an encore, I let out the air in all the tires of the COO's vintage Mustang convertible, which had a tendency to be parked in my reserved Synergy parking space."

After scooping up the stray golden flakes of his spring rolls with his fingers off the table cloth, Fisher asked, "How come you're not flogging Tucker over his gay rights debacle?"

"I intend to win, but I don't intend to win that way. Of course I'm a conservative, but why are we debating gay rights in a school board race? It's a distraction, and I have enough distractions as it is. Let gay people do what they want." Walker gulped down a third of his beer. "Are you gay, Fisher?"

"Who's the reporter here?"

"I didn't think you were gay."

"I am gay."

"But you were a Marine during Vietnam."

"Not exactly the most hospitable place for a closeted homosexual."

"Well, I'll be damned. Were you gay when we were younger?"

"As long as I can remember. You should take this as a compliment, Walker, because if I remember correctly, you were my first crush."

Walker motioned with his hand jokingly for the check. "That is the most flattering, and yet unsettling, thing I have heard since Walker B. Moore Day."

"You're not going to vomit again, are you?" Fisher pretended to exit from their booth. "So there's your answer to why I never ran for office."

"Being gay wouldn't stop you from winning in today's world."

"Not usually a political plus though. I don't think I could emerge from a primary with a Republican or Democratic nomination."

"Run for mayor. It's an open primary. Make your political affiliation 'Houstonian.'"

"I'll be sure to run that advice by your political consultant."

"I fired him. His advice wasn't worth a damn anyway," Walker said. "He and Memorial National and Synergy leaked the gay rights story to the news stations."

"Tucker will lose votes for the controversy. The teachers' union pulled its endorsement."

"The union still refuses to endorse me because I support eliminating tenure in order to fire bad teachers, while giving the excellent and deserving teachers a shot at higher salaries tied to their students' performance in the classroom."

"That's a pity, because I thought your idea was the only unique idea proposed at the debate, and one that could truly help out schools if implemented."

"Me too! At Synergy, we would have called the idea 'innovative,'" Walker said, stabbing his fish with the chopsticks. "I think the proposal to eliminate teacher tenure was why I won the debate."

Fisher knew a draw was a victory in Walker's mind, but what was a loss? Fisher ordered more beers and a fork for Walker.

"I'm convening an emergency board vote tomorrow," Walker said, "to address Dr. Marshall's undisclosed position as a paid consultant for Energy Education. I've had it with conflicts of interest."

"There's a new sheriff in town."

Walker smiled. "I like to think the old one's running again."

— - — - —

Donovan took his ticket from the valet in front of the Houston Museum of Natural Science. "Take good care of it, Carlos, I know your boss."

"Of course, Mr. Kirby," Carlos said.

"How do you know him?" Dr. Green asked Donovan.

"A Green Beret knows people everywhere."

"Why are you called 'Green Berets'?"

"Because President Kennedy authorized our unit special permission to wear whatever headgear we wanted apart from the rest of the military."

"So you could wear a fedora?"

"If Tuck Davis were in command of the unit, perhaps." Donovan smiled at his date and placed his hand on the small of her back, where it seemed to lock in place. In addition to her wry sense of humor, Dr. Green was still a catch. Donovan could not tell if it was his own heart pumping harder or the fluttering of the little birdlike Dr. Green whose body temperature warmed his arm up to his neck as she glanced over her shoulder and smiled. Her wide smile was everything Donovan's crooked half-smile was not.

The senior prom was in the largest wing of the Houston Museum of Natural Science, a multi-floor, open space housing the dinosaur exhibits. A zydeco band played on a temporary stage under the wingspan of a pterodactyl. The hall was decorated like a gambling steamboat with dinosaur card dealers, fusing the official prom theme, Old Man River, with the venue.

"Some theme," Donovan said.

"You think it works?"

"Not at all. Did Tucker Davis have a hand in this?"

"Unfortunately, he was in charge."

Beneath the ribcage of a tyrannosaurus rex, Tucker slow-danced with Duna. There was an odd harmony between the boy and the skeleton that hovered above. Populists and dinosaurs. Both relics of a forgotten past in these go-go nineties. Donovan laughed to himself that thirty years after returning from war he was back in the fight with an eighteen-year-old kid who hailed from an era belonging in a museum. "The first time I met Tucker, he was wearing the same white dinner jacket and bowtie, only he was supervising valets."

"He should be prohibited from supervising anything."

"Ironically, it was at a Synergy event right before they were supposed to buy a controlling stake in my company. If you had told me then that I was going to end up supporting a kid running for school board, I would have told you that you were crazy. The second time I met Tucker was when I busted him out of jail. Now, I finance his radio advertisement campaign."

Dr. Green smiled. "You're the one behind those advertisements?"

"Operation Swooping Crane. Psychological warfare operations, if done right, are highly effective." Donovan raised his plastic prom chalice of Dr Pepper. "*De Oppresso Liber.*"

"What does that mean?"

"Bad Latin for, 'To free the oppressed,'" Donovan said. "The motto of the Special Forces. Catfish might not be out of this race yet. Shall we dance, or talk politics all night?"

"No politics," Dr. Green said, leading Donovan by the hand onto the dance floor.

Ten

Bobby Boudreaux examined the Sunday itinerary Tucker handed him and listened to his anointed son speak in a tongue he understood. Unbelievably to Bobby, Tucker was wearing the Huey Long-era, bronze double-breasted suit that Bobby's chief of staff had briefed him on. Tucker's campaign staff sat silently to the right of Bobby on a sofa in his hotel room. Bobby waited to speak until Tucker finished outlining the campaign plan for the day before the election.

"I'll tell you what I would do," Bobby said. "I would let this whole gay rights controversy pass, and you will win. Go out in front of the cameras today and tell them you can't lose this election unless you're caught in bed with a dead girl or a live boy."

"Honey!" Candy said.

"On second thought, the reporters will eat you up with that line about the live boy after all this gay rights talk. Sidestep any question relating to gays that will tie you to the controversy. Stick to your message of the special tax zones. It is a land-grab people can understand."

"You're right, Governor," Tucker said. "But I can't help but feel Uncle Earl would not have backed down from it."

"Earl Long was crazier than two loons mating. There's

a reason he called himself the Last of the Red Hot Poppas." Bobby plopped two square ice cubes into his drink and swished it around. "The name of the game here is political survival. I've been here before, Tuck. Basing anything off what Uncle Earl would do means you're as crazy as he was."

"You really believe he was crazy?" Tucker asked. "Or was he just labeled crazy, after acting crazy to help black folks get a fair shake?"

Bobby set his drink down and leaned towards Tucker. "No, he was crazy."

"I've never walked away from a fight, Governor, and these gay folks ain't got anyone fighting for them. My backing out of the speaking engagement this afternoon wouldn't be me or this campaign."

Bobby threw up his hands. "When you agreed to speak at this event you didn't have a gay rights political hot potato on your hands either. You walk in there to that part of town—the gay part of town—you're walking into a media alligator pen, and you're the bait. You walk in there and you won't be able to shake this 'gay hugger' label. I lived through the civil rights movement as a politician. You're damn lucky your opponent isn't hitting you harder on this, otherwise we wouldn't even be having this conversation because he'd be leading by twenty points. You got to know when to fight. This is not one of those times. You're running for school board."

"School board," Tucker repeated. He looked at his campaign staff. "It's bigger than me or Duna or Elliott or Carlos. It's what I've aimed for and am still aiming for. But I got a fight, so I got to fight. It's time little folks got the whole hog." He squatted in front of Bobby. "We ain't got no choice—we're the Last Populists, you and me, Governor."

Bobby shook his head. He thought his adopted son, his political heir, a fellow School of Long honor graduate of all people would be receptive to reason. Didn't Tucker want to win? The racists locked Earl Long up in an insane asylum when he made his stand for blacks, and he was the acting governor of the state. Bobby had a crazed fool for a son.

Bobby felt his hand squeezed by his wife, not even a decade older than Tucker. Gathered under the same roof, the Last Populists; one on trial, the other beholden to fight for all little folks. Bobby had fought sentiment his whole life, always making cool political calculations. He controlled a legislature four different terms in office as governor by staying above emotion. It was impossible to remember when politics became more about politics than helping people. He had always played the game better than anyone, one step ahead. The poverty he had risen out of cut both ways, fueling his ascent and lifelong empathy for the poor, but marking him with a greed to beat the moneychangers at their own game and drink from a different cup. What was left of redemption had brought him to a foreign city and the smallest political race of his career. On trial, Bobby stood and proffered to his only political heir what remained, "Against a lifetime of experience, I'm aboard."

Tucker rose to shake hands. "Governor, you were never off the boat."

"This is your one shot, Tucker. I've got to fly back tonight as the deliberation is coming up. Take this," Bobby said, placing his gold and white handkerchief in Tucker's jacket breast pocket. "It's my lucky handkerchief. I never gamble without it."

"I can't accept this, Governor," Tucker said. "You still need it."

"Not where I'm going, Tucker. I wish I would have met you twenty years ago. But I probably wouldn't have listened and we'd both be going to jail."

"Twenty years ago, you were too busy changing American history for little folks."

Bobby put his hand on Tucker's shoulder. "I never really changed much of anything for them, though they kept electing me and giving me a chance to do so. You know Earl lost his fight for black rights, don't you? He died the next year during his comeback race."

"It would take an assassin's bullet to stop this fish with whiskers in this fight for the rights of little folks."

"Which is what got his brother, the Kingfish, in the capitol he built."

An hour later, after a brief stop at Randalson's where Bobby Boudreaux explained the Louisiana Way to Mr. Honeycutt, Joanne Kirby introduced Tucker to a hero's ovation. The art gallery was packed wall to wall with sharply dressed gay couples. The clothes of the mostly male audience were the nicest Tucker had seen while campaigning, not striking him as the wardrobe of little folks. In a strange showing of unity to spotlight the final leg of his campaign to lift little folks up, men held other men's hands. Tucker read from his most recent serialized chapter of his autobiography to the Kirby Contemporary Art Gallery crowd.

It was at the end of my third week when I started to sack less and spend the majority of my time in the break room reading about Huey Long's experiences as a traveling salesman among poor folks during the Great Depression. Like so many of the readers of his autobiography, I was inspired to work even harder to carry on his legacy, and if that meant working less for the Standard Oil of grocery store chains, I was prepared to risk it on behalf of little folks while on the clock.

I began to corner my colleagues when they came in the break room, not allowing them to break and forget about their troubles. I told them about the change that was coming, how even poor boys like us could band together in a fight and beat the corrupt politicians in office. My colleagues might have had to go back out on the line in fifteen minutes and continue working, but I wanted them to know they had a friend in me who was going to stay in the break room and read about Huey Long and take those lessons into the fight against our common enemy, Randalson's. Here, as a kid sacker battling my employer on behalf of my colleagues, was the beginning of my political career. School Board, an elected office not even held by the great Governor, U.S. Senator, and would-be future President, Huey Long, was born at the end of the aisle, where in either paper or plastic I sacked your groceries when not reading Every Man A King *by Huey P. Long in the break room.*

"That was from *Every Kid A King*," Tucker said. "It's the story of a sacker, a sacker like y'all with the odds against him. People advised me against coming out here tonight, speaking to little folks in the Montrose part of town. But if there's one thing the great Governor Bobby Boudreaux taught me, it's not to back down from a fight when you know you are in the right."

The crowd clapped and campaign posters flapped. Bobby Boudreaux stepped forward and raised his right hand. "He's taken down greedy corporations, now help him take down an incumbent," Bobby said to the very crowd he had told Tucker to avoid. "He's your man."

Tucker raised his hands to the ovation and said, "I hope to see y'all downtown this evening at the final rally at Allen's Landing."

— - — - —

Donovan popped open two cans of beer from an ice chest and brought one to Fisher, who reviewed the target intelligence packet Donovan had created from his reconnaissance. Fisher looked up from the unstable porch swing to see a car of youths slowly drive by eyeing Donovan's Land Rover in the driveway. On the porch of Donovan's Old Sixth Ward rental house, a peeling mold-white Victorian home from the late nineteenth century, the cold beer fought the muggy evening to a stalemate in Fisher's body.

"Why do you live here?" Fisher asked.

"Why do you ask? Because the Sixth Ward is run down or because it's dangerous?"

"Both."

Donovan drank from his beer can. "This house is over a hundred years old. You can feel the beating pulse of the city here."

"That's either your heart reacting to the fact that you are about to be robbed or the fault line running through your house's cracked foundation."

"Takes you back to when a can of cold beer after a mission was the greatest thing ever."

"Next to surviving."

"If you were drinking the beer, you had survived. Doesn't it make an old Marine devil dog like you sick to discover that Dr. Marshall was a jarhead, too?"

"You got your good and bad in everything. There are dirtbags everywhere. I seem to remember a fellow Green Beret snake-eater or two of yours being complete cowboys over there in Vietnam—and none of you ever shaved or cut your hair."

"We had to go indigenous, blend in to our environment."

"Show me a picture of one Vietnamese man with a full beard."

"We were Special Forces."

Fisher spit out his beer. "Very *special* indeed."

"You're a real ball-buster for a queen."

Fisher crushed his can. "You're right. You are transporting me back to the enlightened mentality of Nam."

Donovan batted down the incoming crushed can Fisher lobbed at him. "It's crazy to think now how much suck I endured to just complete Special Forces training and how badly I must have wanted to be a Green Beret. Hell, Vietnam was the easy part. Crazy to think Vietnam was the pinnacle of my life."

"I was saying the same thing the other day to Walker Moore. Makes me feel pathetic."

"We must be romanticizing it in our minds."

Fisher opened another beer and recalled how all he wanted to do during his time in Vietnam was get the hell out of Vietnam.

Donovan laughed. "Does this crazy kid remind you of someone?"

"Tucker Davis?"

"I call him 'Hearts and Minds Davis.'"

"He reminds me of the idiots like us who volunteered. The ones who usually get killed."

Donovan sat down next to Fisher on the swing. "I could've gotten out of it, Fisher. I wasn't patriotic, I just felt like I owed it to the country that had given me more than most. That's why I dropped out of law school to volunteer. Had I grown up in just a slightly less wealthy family, like upper middle class instead of in River Oaks, I think I wouldn't have felt so bad about getting my first deferment. Naturally, my parents didn't see it that way and promptly disowned me. Joanne used to tell me that the chip on my shoulder divided the world into men who served and men who didn't serve, and my life was one big dick-measuring contest."

"Oh, the guilt of the landed gentry! Explain then how I ended up in the war with you as well, coming from the untouchable caste of the upper middle class. You realize we're due for another war. Every thirty years since World War I, we have found ourselves in one, after enough time has passed to forget all the lessons learned from the last one."

Donovan put his arm around Fisher and hugged him. "The Cold War is over. In a carefree age with nothing at stake, movie stars are heroes. This is a good thing though, because the guys who don't go to war turn out to be the most hawkish and get that itch when they're our age to strap on the helmet and get their fight on with someone else's kids. Had there not been a draft during Vietnam, no one would have cared at all about us poor bastards half way across the world. In this historical age, there's no one left to fight."

"Don't tell that to Tuck Davis—he's full of fight," Fisher said.

"That son of a bitch is a one-man strategic bombing campaign. I went out on a second date earlier with his school principal to the art gallery, and we could not believe what we saw. Have you seen the signs in Montrose that the gay community has put up?"

"I'm part of the gay community. What are you talking about?"

"A wealthy gay resident financed rainbow-colored signs reading, 'GAYS FOR CATFISH, HE'S A STRAIGHT SHOOTER.'"

— - — - —

The city had named the manatee Huck. And it was at Allen's Landing, where the bayou opened up wide enough for steamboat ships to once turn around and deposit goods downtown, where Huck had lingered for the past two days to growing crowds. Under the cloak of darkened clouds, Elliott and Duna set up the microphone and speakers on the old Port Promenade alongside the thousands of Huck onlookers. Many of the onlookers carried heads of lettuce to feed Huck. News crews on the scene for Huck interviewed Houstonians about the manatee's crossing of a gulf.

Unaware of Huck, Tucker smiled at the sight of the media awaiting the arrival of Catfish, as the taxi carrying him, Fisher, and Governor Boudreaux (minus Candy who had taken a separate taxi to do some shopping at the Galleria with ten thousand dollars in cash her husband gave her) pulled up behind the news vans.

"They still believe," Tucker said, taking a moment to

size up a count of his supporters. "This is an audience fit for you, Governor."

"I'll be damned," Bobby said looking at the mass of people around the bayou and hanging off the bridge. "You know how to organize a rally, Tucker."

Tucker hobbled down the green hill towards the bayou, bowlegs catching on people to spin him around for a handshake. He found Elliott and Duna in a sea of people trying to keep onlookers off the speaker cords.

"Y'all have outdone yourselves," Tucker said. "Look at this crowd. I knew it was a gamble worth taking to send y'all ahead early to set things up here. Have you ever seen so many people for a rally?"

Duna started to speak, but Elliott gave her a brisk shake of the head. "Never," Elliott said.

Fisher and Bobby caught up to Tucker, who climbed atop a replica boat mooring peg on the Port Promenade. "Y'all even found me the perfect stump," Tucker said.

"You're competing, Tuck, with Huck, the manatee," Fisher said.

Tucker carefully turned around on the peg to face the bayou. Under the Sabine Street Bridge, the floating whale of a beast munched on a lettuce head in the brown water. "Too bad Huey and Earl didn't live to see a manatee on the bayou open up for Catfish."

"Maybe you should wait to inject politics until after the manatee submerges for the night, Tucker," Bobby said. "Just like you never speak ill of the dead or live judges, you never overtly mix politics in a nonpolitical environment."

"It ain't but once in a lifetime, Governor, you get a manatee doing the opening act while folks wait for you to show up and stump," Tucker said. "Turn on the microphone, Elliott."

Static screeched. The crowd turned to see Tucker atop the mooring peg at the bayou's edge. Tucker buttoned the lowest front button of his bronze double-breasted suit.

"Ladies and gentlemen, I want to thank y'all for coming out this evening to support me before the election tomorrow. I want to thank Huck too for showing us all what fight is," Tucker said. He pointed to the semi-beached manatee, its flat nose half on the bank, an overweight mermaid gagging on a salad. "He has pushed through an ocean and up polluted channel waters to see this city of ours. Our Huck here full of pluck—despite what the critics and marine biologists say—is not lost!" A regurgitated lettuce head emitted from Huck. "He has come to weigh in and vote. For the future of this city. For school board."

Shouts and a lettuce head wrapped in plastic flew through the air, narrowly missing Tucker's face.

"Pull his microphone." "Get him off the stage." "This is no place for politics." "No one cares." "We're here to watch the manatee."

"I know some of y'all don't agree with me and I understand that. I can muddle up myself these days and get tangled around the axles," Tucker said, confusing the outcry with his recent comments on gays he had made to the press. "If you're going to throw lettuce, at least take off the plastic covering first for Huck—"

A second unwrapped lettuce head exploded on Tucker's forehead, knocking his fedora off. The mob clapped and shouted.

"Shut up." "I hope Huck eats your hat." "No one is listening." "Enough." "You look gay in that suit."

Tucker stepped off the mooring peg to pick up his hat before a wind could take it into the bayou. He spit out the salty, grassy taste of the cheap, dry lettuce that stuck to his lips. He wiped the remnants of the lettuce head from his face with Bobby's lucky handkerchief. Next to Tucker, Fisher flicked pieces of lettuce off his shirt. Seeing that Fisher had been wounded too, Tucker passed the handkerchief to Fisher and climbed back atop the mooring stump to face the dissenters. Boos pelted the ear of Tucker. He heard them, deep and stinging, and thought of Earl Long on the legislature floor fighting for the rights of blacks. Had his brother the Kingfish ever been stung this painfully before his hometown people? Still, Tucker looked out at the crowd of his final rally and thought how the Share Our Wealth Coalition had come a long way from the signatures of four hundred of his classmates. If his stubborn friends did not want to be led to water, then driven by the tongue of Catfish they would be. It would take more than an assassin's bullet to fell a bull catfish of destiny. Tucker made eye contact with the expressionless face of Bobby. Encouraged by the shared determination he saw within Governor Boudreaux and a desire to shield his wounded friend under assault from a few bigots in the crowd, a remounted Tucker violently whipped about the fedora in his left hand like he was riding a bull through the sky.

"Y'all better have a whole cart of them lettuce heads, friends," Tucker said, "because it's going to take that just to start on me! I did not come here to preach gay rights to y'all, but them folks got rights, too. I ain't ever even been gay or known me many gays in my life, but that don't mean I can't defend them. They're just like you and me and that manatee there. You think I got a say in being attracted to my pretty little girlfriend there?" Tucker pointed his fedora at Duna.

Duna looked at Elliott. "I'm his girlfriend?"

"Well," Tucker bellowed, "I don't! It just so happens that—like politics—that is what I was built for I reckon. Ain't got any control over this, and neither do the gays. One day all you piss-ant lettuce-heads are going to wake up and ask, 'Why is my brain no more advanced than this head of lettuce I keep throwing at that crazy Catfish?'"

"What's wrong with you?" "We have a problem with you, not gays!" "Put a sock in it." "You are crazy." "Are you off your medicine?"

The news crews moved in to capture the spectacle. Tucker took no notice and continued on with his torrent as the crowd stirred and his mind remade the Port Promenade into the legislature floor, gay folks as black folks, and a mad Tucker an insane Earl Long.

"Well, I might be crazy, but at least I ain't crazy enough to throw away my only lettuce head," Tucker shouted. His right hand tapped his temple. "Forty years ago they said Earl Long was crazy, too, when he stood up for the black man. Called our Uncle Earl a mad dog fighting for the rights of little folks. They locked him up in a mental hospital instead of listening to him, but history has shown us Governor Earl Long was *right*! Vote me down and out of office if y'all have to, but this is what I believe is right. Y'all got to recognize that gays are human beings too! They ain't just got fight, they got rights!"

Before a cart of lettuce heads could knock the Last Populist into the bayou, the clouds cracked and two months of pent-up rain fell on the drought-stricken city. Gulf winds and flashes of lightning sent the remnants of the crowd home.

— - — - —

"Why is your indicted governor being interviewed on television like a homeless person under the Sabine Street Bridge?" Dr. Davis asked his wife.

Over the sharkskin suited shoulder of Governor Boudreaux, three homeless people sought shelter from the rain under the cover of the bridge. Mrs. Davis stopped cutting onions and switched the volume on to hear what the tall, black-haired female reporter was saying. Dr. Davis laughed at the level to which Louisiana Governor Bobby Boudreaux had sunk, stooping to associate with bayou bums for sympathy.

"What we witnessed here today was an act of courage we haven't seen or felt in politics since Earl Long defied the legislature in my own state forty years ago," Bobby Boudreaux said. "This kid has it all."

Dr. Davis felt his own heart sink to a new low. He clung to his wife's hand.

"Governor," the reporter said, "there were many people who said the speech by Tucker Davis on gay rights was completely unwarranted. They were here to observe the manatee, not be challenged on their political stances. The impression they had was that candidate Tucker Davis was off in another world."

"He is in another world," Dr. Davis said to the screen.

"Quiet," Mrs. Davis said.

"He's crazy all right, but he's the Last Populist," Bobby Boudreaux said. "That's no small thing, as we saw today."

The camera moved back to the female reporter who said, "I also have here with me veteran *Chronicle* reporter Fisher K. Hughes who has been covering this story since it began and who has an announcement of his own. Fisher, tell our viewers what you told us."

"So this is the idiot who has fueled this firestorm," Dr. Davis said.

"I like his articles," Mrs. Davis said.

"Announce to us all you are an idiot!" Dr. Davis screamed at the screen.

"I'm Fisher Hughes, I'm gay," Fisher said. "And I'm a candidate for mayor."

Dr. Davis sat down on the kitchen floor. Onscreen, the three homeless people cheered Tucker's name and recounted a feast of crawfish they shared with Catfish.

Eleven

Reinstated as a student, Tucker had to spend the first part of Election Day in class, anxiously awaiting the three o'clock bell. He spent it trying to shore up the Jefferson High School senior class vote and fine-tuning his final assault on the district. Outside, rain continued to sweep through the city. After school, Tucker had Elliott bus people from Shady Oaks to the polls. Helping organize the transportation of supporters was the Silver Fox, who had notified Tucker that Memorial National, in a vindictive swipe after the Memorial TIRZ defeat, would not be providing any bus service on Monday due to "unforeseen maintenance." Carlos was stationed at Randalson's to canvass the after-work crowd of shoppers for votes. He operated under a temporary lift of the moratorium on campaigning on store property after Tucker had Governor Boudreaux squeeze Mr. Honeycutt.

Duna and her father were assigned the Spring Branch commercial sector. With the aid of the same twenty illegal Mexican immigrants Tucker had hired to pass out fliers the second week of the campaign, Duna oversaw campaigning at intersections deemed strategic by Tucker. Dragooned "one last time" for Election Day, the Brothers Curry were stationed a hundred yards away from the entrance of the elementary school where they had once been the only black students. They passed out a circular telling voters how to vote the straight Tucker Davis Ticket, a ticket consisting of Tucker Davis and a list of his other nicknames and aliases, so voters had no doubt that the catfish they were voting for was Tuck Davis.

Throughout the afternoon and evening outside Walker B. Moore Auditorium, Tucker's bowlegs acted as a vortex, each new voter given the full Catfish Davis treatment: head-on entrapment by the splitting legs, a two-handed grip of the voting hand, then an arm around the shoulders and a denouncement of his opponent, with Tucker's guarantee of an Every Kid A King Program for the Memorial Independent School District. In the rain, it was a hurried exchange. The saturated candidate would come to life with the newly saturated voter trying to escape. When there was no voter around, Tucker tried out lines for the press conference he would hold to announce his victory. Striking the right chord of confidence coupled with honesty about the direness of the school district state was essential. The first one hundred days of Every Kid A King were pivotal, Tucker stressed internally to his campaign team. His administration had much to do in little time.

Tucker wondered where his future constituents were tonight. The rain, unfortunately, was apparently discouraging some of the less determined school board voters. The fate of the school board on the line, they must be waiting for a break in the weather. During a smoke break, one of the voting booth officials told Tucker that turnout was low. Tucker assured her the weather would not stop the people from voting in the landmark school board election. It was them, not Catfish, Tucker told her, who filled the administration building the night of the TIRZ vote. The people preserved this land from ruin. He was just the Last Populist. Without the people, a populist was not much, even the Last Populist.

The voting turnout, Tucker assumed, was larger in the Tucker Davis strongholds in Spring Branch, strongholds even more crucial in light of the recent turmoil with the Cajun bloc. After catching Tucker out of uniform staging an impromptu final rally outside the opera following the failure at Allen's Landing, J.D. Thibodaux had fired Tucker from Lagniappe Valet along with Tucker's pals he had put on the payroll, throwing the Cajun vote up in the air. With an overdrawn campaign account and no way to shake down money by overcharging at valet events, there were no funds for a massive crawfish boil or barbeque to draw out supporters on Election Day.

Earlier in the evening, Tucker had given an interview to the black-haired television reporter, but all she wanted to talk about was gay rights. He wondered how much this controversy was hurting his campaign. Governor Boudreaux had told Tucker not to address it—no matter that there were little folks getting walked on. But Fisher Hughes was gay—the first gay person Tucker had ever known—and Fisher was a damn good man in a fight. It just would not be right not to fight, Tucker figured, as a candidate for school board.

Through the rain, Tucker saw the man in the black suit running towards the auditorium from the parking lot. Tucker's legs shot out as if two slugs from a bucktoothed double-barreled shotgun as he raced in his soaked bronze suit of armor to meet the supporter before he reached the buffer inside where candidates were banned from campaigning. The supporter stopped before the imminent collision with the split-apart legs of the crashing downhill racer. The supporter was Walker Moore.

Walker looked at his drenched challenger guarding the entrance to his auditorium. Both wore the same suit as the day when Tucker commenced war in the same venue. In the slanted rain, Walker contemplated, whether on top of all the other shame, if he should lose, could Tucker change the name of his auditorium? Walker's disgrace complete, what procedure would Tucker use to achieve it? Water hitting him from every angle, Walker determined he would employ whatever countermeasures necessary in his last lame duck month on school board to prevent such an act. It pained Walker to consider what his campaign would have been like had he only consulted Winston Churchill from the outset.

"Came to cast your ballot in your own auditorium?" Tucker asked.

"Voted earlier," Walker said. "Thought I'd finish up the campaign on this side of the tracks at my alma mater."

"Your base."

"My base. What about your base? I thought you would be in Spring Branch."

"I wanted to concentrate over here and rope in the fence-sitters. Not a lot of people."

"There was next to no one at the schools in Spring Branch where I was bouncing around most of the day."

Tucker and Walker moved under the overhang, protected from the rain. "You heard about Dr. Marshall, I take it?" Walker asked.

"I read about the consulting contract in the paper," Tucker said.

"He resigned earlier this morning."

"Before I fired him."

"Before I fired him." Walker thought about it a moment and conceded, "Or before you fired him."

Tucker smiled and offered a handshake. "May the better man win."

"You already beat me on the Memorial TIRZ."

"I would've beat you," Tucker said, "but you wisely voted it down. You found your little folks to fight for just in time."

"Your double-crossing Earl Long voting wisdom provided additional moral guidance," Walker said, shaking Tucker's hand. "Looks like I will be speaking at your graduation next week now, because Dr. Marshall sure won't be."

"You can warm up the crowd for me then, because I'm giving the class profile speech. I found out this morning from Dr. Green."

"I'll do that for you, win or lose tonight."

"You think people aren't turning out tonight because of the gay issue? Besides Fisher Hughes, who was here for a while, the only other reporter was a woman wanting to talk about the gay rights issue."

Walker stepped out into the rain, his hands raised and palms up, his back to the Walker B. Moore auditorium. "What you got to remember is that Houstonians have a short memory. Call it, 'amnesia for the not new.' Next week they won't remember the gay rights fight, and they have already forgotten about the tax incremental reinvestment zone fight. Mayor Whiting and the rest want me to reintroduce it for a vote. It would probably pass if I did."

Tucker joined Walker in the rain. "You're wrong about this town. I might be voted down, but the little folks here understand history well. That's why this has been such a close race. How come you didn't hammer me harder on the gay rights controversy?"

Walker twirled to face Tucker. "I'm running for reelection to school board. Yet I've got a runaway, overpaid consultant disobeying my orders and my own friends and colleagues attempting to manipulate me. I'd like to win one on my terms even more than I'd like to take you down on some controversial issue."

"You should've, coach," Tucker said, smiling at the amateur political mistake. "I would've dynamited you over a stand like that to win."

"You did, Tucker. It was called the Memorial Tax Incremental Reinvestment Zone."

"For little folks, I had to beat you bloody on that until you bled Louisiana Long," Tucker said. "For the little folks."

— - — - —

Tucker, wearing his red graduation robe over his bronze double-breasted suit, wrote at his bedroom desk on the backside of an extra campaign flier.

Dear Governor Boudreaux,

I am pained to have read the verdict of your unfair trial, if you could call that circus a trial. My mom explained to me that you will get to appeal it and should get off once you get another judge to hear your story. It is a story worth hearing. Although your luck might be bad at the moment, there's no way you will get a worse judge this time around. Once you get a new trial, the people will remember what you did for them as Governor of Louisiana and wake up from their sleeping state and vote you in again. I want to thank you and tell you I will never forget you coming down here to campaign with me.

I am sorry to inform you that I lost as well. Walker Moore ended up beating me for school board by a little less than one hundred votes, 2,051 to 1,968. Even my opponent said I should've followed your advice on dealing with the gay rights issue. I know y'all are right, but I might have won if I just hadn't lost the Cajun vote by getting fired the night before Election Day. Mr. Thibodaux has a lot of influence in my Texan county among the Cajun population.

I know you never lost in your career, Governor Boudreaux. And had this trial been an election, you would have won. But I did lose. That said, so did the Kingfish and Uncle Earl when they first ran for office. So I aim to get back out there politicking with my new lucky handkerchief in my pocket. Hell, I'm going to stump right now, to give a speech thanking you and maybe get myself a few future votes. Because there are still little folks out there, and we hear them. And when I get elected, I'm going to have to call on you one last time to swear me in and maybe say a few words at my inauguration. Every Kid A King.

Your son,
Tuck Catfish Davis

"Tucker," Mrs. Davis said at the door. "Elliott is here to drive you to graduation."

"Be there in a minute," Tucker said. Tucker took the photo of Huey Long off his wall and wrote on it:

The good people of the State of Louisiana ain't ever had themselves a better friend than Governor Bobby Boudreaux, the Cajun King, and the Last Populist to the little folks and working man over three decades of Every Man A King!

"It's your graduation," Mrs. Davis said. "You can't be late."

Tucker opened the door and handed his mom the letter, the photo, and a campaign sign and asked her if, as a graduation gift, she would mail it all in a package to Governor Boudreaux.

"Don't you look nice," Mrs. Davis said. "Did you remember to take a copy of your speech?"

"Is the Kingfish a friend of the poor?"

— - — - —

Seated in the row behind the graduating students in Walker B. Moore Auditorium, Fisher listened to his old classmate of the same name. Fisher took no notes and his audio recorder had been left at home. At the podium stood Walker, dressed in a tan suit and a blue bowtie with small white polka dots, what Walker referred to as the "Churchill pattern" before the ceremony. A week before, Walker had offered Fisher the commencement speaker honor. Fisher refused as a declared mayoral candidate and insisted Walker should bestow it upon himself and share the stage with his former opponent and fellow president, Tucker. Fisher pondered the idea of the Last Wildcatter, now without a job at Synergy, running Fisher's campaign for mayor.

"Let me congratulate those of you who earned a gold tassel on your cap for graduating *magna cum laude*," Walker said.

Applause flowed through the auditorium. The acoustics were great, Fisher admitted to himself. To Fisher's right, the Silver Fox and Donovan clapped in their seats.

"Yet, to the rest of you, don't let the absence of a gold tassel take away from your moment as you walk across this stage today," Walker said. "I know of at least two people from this very school without one. One of them was a classmate of mine at Jefferson, and he's now running for mayor. A former senior class president, he felt the responsibility of a leader to volunteer for a war when few of us—so busy with our own priorities—even bothered to locate Vietnam on a map. He would later serve our great city by protecting Houston from fools like me who would tear it down to build it up in an endless cycle that truly built nothing.

"The other is a classmate of yours here onstage with me today, and the toughest politician I have ever faced or heard about. Yes, Tucker Davis, the one you call Catfish, nearly beat me last week for school board. Honestly, he probably deserved to beat me. At times it was like being tied to a whipping post, and I hated him for it—still resent some of those stinging remarks. The kid took down city hall and some of the most powerful business interests in the city. But when he had the chance to run from some controversial stances and finish me off, Tucker stood by them and fought for people he thought deserved to have someone fight for those of a different stripe. That is courage, though pure political folly. Like another little man long ago, the Last Lion of Britain, Winston S. Churchill, who was just crazy enough to make his people see themselves the way he saw them . . ."

What was this sudden obsession with Churchill? Fisher would have to address this with the man he wanted to run his mayoral campaign. If Fisher wanted a biased historian as a campaign manager, he had Tucker. Fisher loosened his tie. The audience applauded the recipients of the newly created district scholarships endowed by Donovan Kirby: the Huey P. Long Scholarship for Unconventional Academic Excellence awarded to Dunazade Shari, the Earl K. Long Scholarship for the Asymmetrically Talented to Elliott Taylor, and the Bobby Boudreaux Scholarship for Clandestine Leadership to Carlos Ortega.

"That was a nice gesture from an old pirate like you," Fisher said to Donovan.

"I didn't have any choice," Donovan said. "Less than twenty-four hours after I fended off the hostile takeover of Sundance, Tucker blackmailed me by convincing Dr. Green to not go on a third date with me until I helped the class leave a legacy. He's the pirate."

"May you enjoy your moment today, and if you ask yourself anything, ask, 'What legacy will you leave?'" Walker addressed the crowd.

Walker walked over and sat next to Tucker onstage. Fisher could see they laughed at something Tucker pointed out in the program. Fisher checked his program and discovered they had reversed the speaking order. A murmur broke out in the crowd as Tucker rose. He took off his mortarboard graduation cap to pull out his folded speech in the top of his cap.

"Class of 1999," Tucker said. He waited a beat. "They saved the best for last."

Fisher clapped and others joined. The Silver Fox and Donovan yelled Tucker's name.

"I got a speech here," Tucker said, holding it up. "It's a fine speech about politics, if you happen to like politics. But I ain't going to read it to y'all, not at this graduation anyway."

Fisher checked his program again that stated: CLASS OF 1999 PROFILE BY TUCKER DAVIS. There was not supposed to be politics in a class profile, Fisher knew, having delivered a class profile thirty-five years earlier as class president. Onstage, Dr. Green looked like she was praying that the ceremony would not end the way it had every other time Tucker took the stage in the new auditorium. A glimpse of Tucker's bronze double-breasted suit flashed through the V-shaped opening at the collar of the graduation robe.

"The speech I aim to make is one about this class, the Class of 1999, best damn class in the West," Tucker said.

The graduating student section roared. Fisher knew this would not help the speaker stay off politics. Dr. Green was as still as a statue onstage. Edwin and Kingsley Curry stood up in the student section and mockingly raised their right fists for solidarity.

"I'll put this class up against any class that has ever walked this stage," Tucker said, pointing at the new stage that his graduating class would be the first to walk across in the Walker B. Moore Auditorium.

Wanting to urge the people to stop cheering, Fisher shifted in his seat and thought, *this is how it starts.* Fisher spied Elliott and Duna turn to each other two rows ahead. To Fisher's left, the face of the Most Outstanding Teacher of the Year, Mrs. Bridge, ran white as the whale she had assigned Tucker to study.

"Hell," the senior class president stated, "we'll spot you an extra valedictorian and a couple student council class representatives, and we'll still take your class on. The Jefferson High School Class of 1999 has fight. It's a class legacy that ain't just about surviving, it's about doing the right thing in the fight. They're going to call us crazy, and I reckon we just might be crazy, but if our class legacy of fight is what makes us crazy, then call us crazy!

"Because they called Governor Earl Long crazy before our Class of 1999 came along, but y'all know what he did? He fought for the little folks of Louisiana with all he had until his political enemies jailed him in a mental hospital. Even tied up Uncle Earl in one of those white suits. Only thing about our crazy Uncle Earl, he was still the governor, so he fired the director of the state hospital system on a conference call from a phone inside the insane asylum and replaced the director with a loyal political supporter who declared Earl mentally sane and released! What did Earl do? He came back and ran until he fell over and died at a campaign site. Just like Governor Long, this class doesn't quit a fight, even if it means we're crazy. Hell, we have the first ever winner of the Earl K. Long Scholarship for the Asymmetrically Talented here in this class. If all that ain't a class legacy, then I don't much know what a class legacy is."

Later, when the Class of 1999 received their diplomas after an anecdote about Huey Long's recipe for good collard greens in what Fisher supposed was a metaphor for life, Fisher found the school board candidate of the people outside talking to his mother and father. The Last Populist had traded the graduation hat for his Uncle Remy's fedora hat, which clashed with his red robe.

"I want y'all to meet the next Mayor of Houston," Tucker said, introducing Fisher to his parents.

"Such an honor," Mrs. Davis said. "I just loved your stories on the school board election. You know you have the Davis vote."

"I saw your announcement on television," Dr. Davis said, "and said, 'At least he'll be too busy to write articles about our son.'"

"That sounds like an endorsement," Fisher said.

"What endorsements have you gathered so far?" Tucker asked.

"None so far, Tuck," Fisher said.

"What the hell have you been doing for a week?" Tucker asked. "Who's running your campaign?"

"Presently, me," Fisher said. "I was thinking about asking Walker Moore since he resigned from Synergy."

"You might have to fire him, or at least demote him, because I ain't got anything but time to get you elected. You can't tell me Catfish ain't the best friend the gays ever had here. I'm a populist, the last of them—until there's another!"

"I thought you were going to college in New Orleans."

"Hell, my conditional acceptance off the wait list doesn't force me to report until the fall. And it is just down the bayou in New Orleans. I can always hop a freighter or make my way by hitching a ride on the hump of Huck if I have to—and that's why God gave us manatees, I reckon, to race them against keelboats all the way down river to New Orleans. Besides, Donovan Kirby offered me a summer internship at his company in a new unconventional division, Talent Deployed Across Houston. It looks like I just spotted my first talent, populist Fisher Hughes."

"I don't know, Tucker," Fisher said. "I can't encourage you to jump into another race."

"Dammit, son," Tucker said to Fisher, "I won't always be here to light a fire under your ass. I know you haven't forgotten everything you learned as senior class president. We're not talking about any race—we're talking about seating a goddamn mayor in Houston!"

Behind Tucker, Dr. Davis moved his hand back and forth across his throat to convey his stance on his son's latest plan. Fisher attempted to steer the conversation off politics and back to the formal graduation atmosphere with less cursing, but Tucker already had one arm around Fisher's shoulder and was spinning a way to make being gay a political advantage, leading him down, down, down in the direction of the bayou.

ACKNOWLEDGMENTS

I would especially like to thank Kirby Thornton for her unflinching support and her time spent reading over each draft, and Elliott Walthall, who was there from the beginning in the role of best friend and fellow writer. I would also like to thank Mikey Wise, Justin Springer, Russ Fusco, Erik Dane, and Mike Quinn. And of course Bruce Rutledge and all of the people at Chin Music Press for being enthusiastic believers in the novel. Lastly, I owe a great debt to the city and people of my hometown of Houston, and my former military colleagues who somehow managed to keep me alive to write a novel that is dedicated in their honor.